ALIENS Vol. 1
ISBN# 1-878574-08-6

Published by Dark Horse Comics Inc.
2008 S.E. Monroe
Milwaukie, OR 97222

June 1990

ALIENS ™

ALIENS

written by
MARK VERHEIDEN

illustrated by
MARK A. NELSON

lettered by
WILLIE SCHUBERT

INSPIRED BY THE DESIGNS AND CREATIONS OF H.R. GIGER
Based on the characters and events in theTwentieth Century Fox film

special thanks to:
Kathleen Aiken   Tom Baxa   Jeff Butler   Bob Dvorak   Jeff Easley   Scott Hill
Laurie Jenkins   Anitia Nelson   Pam North   Ron Randall   Gil Rocha   Mike Schneider

publisher
MIKE RICHARDSON

editor
RANDY STRADLEY

operations director
NEIL HANKERSON

production manager
CHRIS CHALENOR

production
JIM BRADRICK   JIM SPIVEY   JACK POLLOCK

controller
BRAD HORN

administrative assistants
DEBBIE BYRD   JERRY PROSSER

Ten years later...

DO YOU WANT TO TALK ABOUT LAST NIGHT?

WHY? IT WON'T MAKE ANY DIFFERENCE.

GIVE ME A TRY.

"IT STARTED WHEN MY FRIEND CARLY FOUND AN OLD DISC ABOUT CAMPING--YOU KNOW, THE *REAL* STUFF, ABOUT THE REAL LAND. THE DISC TALKED ABOUT THE CAMPING FIRE AND SING-AROUND SONGS."

"WE 'BORROWED' A CRAWLER AND DROVE OUT TO ONE OF THE REMOTE GENERATOR BUILDINGS."

"WE COULDN'T LIGHT A FIRE, BUT WE PLUGGED A CRAWLER HEATER INTO ONE OF THE BATTERY OUTLETS AND GOT CLOSE TO KEEP WARM."

I'M FREEZING! WHO'S IDEA WAS THIS?

YOURS POWER-DRAIN!

"I REMEMBER THINKING HOW MUCH I LIKED BEING THERE, AWAY FROM THE COLONY AND THE MACHINES-- JUST ME AND MY FRIENDS."

WHAT ELSE DID THEY DO ON THE DISC, CARLY?

THEY BURNED RATIONS OVER A FIRE, WHICH SEEMED KINDA DUMB. AND SOMETIMES THEY...

SOMETIMES THEY TOLD STORIES. SCARY STORIES.

"CARLY WENT FIRST. IT WAS SOMETHING ABOUT VAMPIRES AND WITCHES AND MONSTERS. I KNEW IT WAS STRAIGHT OUT OF THE DISC LIBRARY, BUT IT DIDN'T MATTER. WITH THE WIND AND THE RAIN AND THE HUM OF THE HEATER IT WAS AS SCARY AS ANY VIDEO."

GOD! I HATE VAMPIRES!

SHHHH!

"...AND THEN...HE DRANK... ALL OF HER... *BLOOD*!!"

"ABOUT THEN THE HEATER STOPPED WORKING. MAYBE IT WAS A SHORT. EVERYTHING TURNED COLD AND BLUE AND I STARTED TO SHIVER."

YOUR TURN, NEWT. WHAT'S THE SCARIEST THING YOU EVER SAW?

NO. I WANT TO GO BACK!

IT WAS *YOUR* IDEA, NEWT. DON'T CHICKEN OUT NOW--!

"I KNEW IF I DIDN'T TELL THEY'D NEVER GO BACK."

A WITCH? DON'T BE STUPID!

YOU KNOW SOMETHING SCARIER THAN THAT! TELL US!

OKAY, OKAY. I KNEW A STORY ABOUT A REAL SCARY WITCH AND--

PL--PLEASE-- CAN'T WE GO BACK--

TELL IT!

"I STARTED TO GET MAD AT THEM, PICKING ON ME LIKE THAT, ALL I WANTED TO DO WAS GO HOME. I DECIDED TO TELL THEM THE SCARIEST STORY I KNEW."

BETTER!

THERE ARE THESE-- *THINGS*-- THAT LIVE IN SPACE. THEY LIVE TO FEED-- AND TO HATE.

THEY HAVE ACID FOR BLOOD AND SKIN AS HARD AS HULL STEEL. YOU DON'T SEE THEM UNTIL THEY'RE ON TOP OF YOU. AND THEN ALL YOU SEE ARE THE *TEETH*, GLITTERING LIKE *SPARKS* AS THEY *SNAP*--

I--I DON'T FEEL SO GOOD--

MAYBE THEY'RE FROM ANOTHER WORLD. OR MAYBE THEY JUST EXIST IN THE BLACK HELL OF SPACE, FEEDING ON ANYTHING THEY FIND. IT DOESN'T MATTER.

NOTHING MATTERS BUT THOSE *TEETH*, SNAPPING SHUT ON BONE AND BRAIN TEARING, CUTTING, CRUSHING--

BUT IT DOESN'T END IN DEATH.

THEY USE WHAT'S LEFT FOR BREEDING, BURROWING INTO THE TISSUE, SPREADING LIKE CANCER, UNTIL THE PARASITE IS *WHOLE*, UNTIL THE *HATE* CAN BUILD AGAIN AND AGAIN AND--

MAG! WHAT'S WRONG?

SOMETHING--IS--AAA-- *AAAAAGGGGH!*

OH GOD, NO!

I DON'T FEEL--

NOT AGAIN! NOT AGAIN!

"I GUESS THAT'S WHEN YOU FOUND ME IN THE HALL, SCREAMING."

NEWT! WAKE UP! YOU'RE DREAMING!

IF YOU'RE FEELING BETTER I'LL *LOOSEN* THE STRAPS.

YOU CAN DO ANYTHING YOU WANT. IT WON'T STOP THE DREAMS. *NOTHING* CAN STOP THE DREAMS.

9

HICKS! FRONT AND CENTER!

GIVE IT A REST, PERKINS. I'VE STILL GOT 24 HOURS TO SERVE ON THE D&D CHARGES.

YOU *WISH*, PAL. MUCH AS I'D LIKE TO SLAM YOU BACK FOR ANOTHER CYCLE, YOUR HIGH RANKING FRIENDS HAVE OTHER PLANS.

IT'S ABOUT TIME! I'M NOT SAFE IN HERE WITH HIM!

I DON'T *HAVE* ANY HIGH RANKING FRIENDS.

HE'S *SICK*, MAN-- YOU DON'T KNOW *WHAT* HE'S GOT INSIDE HIM--!

SOUNDS LIKE YOU DON'T HAVE ANY *FRIENDS*, PERIOD.

WATCH THE DISC AND REPORT TO COLONEL STEPHENS AT 0800. HELL, MAYBE YOU COULD EVEN TRY AND LOOK LIKE A SOLDIER.

I'LL TRY IF YOU'LL TRY.

"I KNEW IT WAS A BAD SIGN WHEN PERKINS ACTUALLY OPENED THE CELL. I LEARNED A LONG TIME AGO--*NOBODY* GOES OUT ON A LIMB UNLESS THEY WANT SOMETHING. SOMEBODY MUST HAVE WANTED ME *BAD*."

"THEY STILL CALL THEM THE COAST GUARD, EVEN THOUGH THE COAST THEY'RE GUARDING IS THREE OR FOUR HUNDRED MILES OUT IN SPACE.

"IT WAS A LOT CHEAPER TO ABANDON A SHIP THAN RETRO-FIT AND REFUEL, ESPECIALLY THE OLD STYLE NUCLEAR JOBS. A LOT OF THE INDUSTRIALS JUST DUMPED THEM IN DECAYING ORBIT, WAITING FOR GRAVITY AND ATMOSPHERIC BURN-UP TO SOLVE THEIR PROBLEM.

"THAT WORKED UNTIL ONE OF THE FLAMERS CRASHED HALF-INTACT NEAR A COFFEE PLANTATION ON THE ISLAND OF HAWAII. THE RADIATION KILLED THE INDIGENOUS POPULATION AND MADE IT DAMN NEAR IMPOSSIBLE TO FIND A GOOD CUP OF 'KONA'.

"SO NOW THE COAST GUARD TAGS THE FLOATERS AND BLASTS THEM BEFORE THEY CAN DECAY INTO THE ATMOSPHERE. KEEPS THE WORLD SAFE AND GIVES THE GUARD BOYS SOMETHING TO DO BETWEEN POKER GAMES."

PROBE AWAY.

11

SEE THAT, LYLE? THE DOOR'S BULGING *OUT.* LIKE SOMEBODY WAS TRYING TO BLOW IT FROM THE *INSIDE.*

THAT'S CRAZY. THAT'S A *DRYDOCK* PORT. OPEN *THAT* IN SPACE AND IT'S BYE-BYE ATMOSPHERE.

15:32:10

YEAH, AND THE *PILOT'S POD* IS GONE, TOO.

3...2...1... KAPOW.

GOOD SHOT. TAKE 'ER IN.

15:33:08

OH, *JESUS*--

STUPID BASTARD WASN'T EVEN WEARING A PRESSURE SUIT--LIKE HE WAS COMMITTING *SUICIDE*--

HURRY IT UP. THIS THING'S STARTING TO HEAT UP.

15:34:55

KILL US ALL

IS THAT BLOOD? I THINK THAT'S *BLOOD,* MAN!

I'VE SEEN THIS BEFORE--IT'S LIKE MEGA-CLAUSTROPHOBIA OR SOMETHING--ONE GUY SNAPS AND TAKES THE REST WITH HIM.

15:36:20

LOUNGE

FINALLY GOT A READ ON THE VESSEL. STANDARD TYPE FIVE, NUKE ENGINES, OLD STYLE TRANSMITTER--DID A LOT OF DEEP SPACE TIME. TOTAL BUCKET. NO WONDER THEY DITCHED IT--

WAIT A MINUTE. I'M GETTING SOMETHING ON THE MOTION DETECTOR.

15:38:49

12

LOOK AT THOSE HOLES. WHAT THE HELL *DOES* THAT?

THREE METERS AND CLOSING.

WE DON'T HAVE TIME FOR MYSTERIES. HULL TEMPERATURE'S UP ANOTHER 50 DEGREES. IT'S GONNA START FLARING ANY SECOND.

15:40:01

--BACK OFF! BACK OFF!

IT'S JUST A DAMN CARGO CARRIER, MAN!

15:40:12

WE MUST HAVE JOLTED IT WHEN WE BURNED THE AIRLOCK.

LOOK, THE MANUAL SAYS CHECK FOR SALVAGE. I DON'T SEE ANY SALVAGE. OK. SO *PLANT* THE DAMN NUKES AND *DUST* THE DAMN THING.

15:55:06

WAIT A MINUTE-- I'M PICKING UP SOMETHING *ELSE*-- RIGHT ON TOP OF THE PROBE.

THE WHOLE SHIP'S PROBABLY *CRAWLING* WITH AUTOMATES. C'MON, MOVE IT!

BOMB 327-3 DVORAK 10-CA
ON--

15:59:99

DID WE GET A COMPLETE HISTORY FROM THE ONBOARD? I THINK COMMAND'S GOING TO WANT TO SEE SOME HARD COPY ON THIS TUB.

I PULLED EVERYTHING IN THE QUEUE. THAT BETTER DO IT, 'CAUSE AS THEY SAY DOWN SOUTH--

HASTA LA VISTA!

PROBE TWENTY METERS AND CLOSING.

DAMN, THESE CONTROLS ARE SLUGGISH.

YEAH? THAT'S WHY WE STILL HAVE JOBS! COMPENSATE, BOY! COMPENSATE!

TEN METERS AND CLOS--TOO FAST SLOW IT DOWN, FOR CHRIST'S SAKE!

I'M TRYING-- SOMETHING'S INHIBITING THE LEFT RETRO!

AIRLOCK DOORS OPEN.

I'M KICKING SOME TECH ASS IF THEY MESSED WITH THE RETRO SYS--

WHAT IN THE HELL--?

IT'S IMPOSSIBLE--

16:03:03

14

THAT'S TOTAL VACUUM-- AND IT'S *ALIVE*--!

THIS IS PROBE SHIP DUTTON-- WE--WE'VE PULLED SOMETHING IN FROM--

MAYBE IT'S SOME KIND OF-- PARASITE-- OR--

THAT'S NO PARASITE--

--OH MY GOD!

IT'S GOING TO--

GAHHHHHYYYYY---*

"I KNEW IT WAS ONLY A MATTER OF TIME BEFORE IT HAPPENED. THAT'S WHY THE MARINES NEVER KICKED ME OUT OF THE CORPS. THEY KNEW IT, TOO.

"I SAW A GUY TEAR HIS SUIT ONCE. HE HAD TIME FOR ONE SCREAM--THEN HIS BLOOD BEGAN TO *BOIL*--

"ALL THINGS CONSIDERED, THOSE BOYS ON THE COAST GUARD SHIP WERE *LUCKY.*

"PROBE SHIPS WEREN'T DESIGNED TO WITHSTAND A HULL BREACH. THE ALIEN WAS CLEVER, BUT NOT THAT CLEVER.

"THE SHIP EXPLODED, TAKING THE ALIEN SON OF A BITCH WITH IT. BUT PROOF OF THE ONE MEANT THERE WERE MORE.

SHIP TERMINATED.
NO SURVIVORS.

"WHAT WAS THE OLD PHRASE? 'WHERE THERE'S SMOKE, THERE'S FIRE.' YEAH-- THE FIRES OF *HELL.*"

YOU'RE LATE.

GET OFF MY BACK, SALVAJE. YOU'RE LUCKY I'M HERE AT ALL.

Excerpts from the book *The Evolution of Television* by Emmett Webster, DH Press, 2057: "Commercial television as it was known in the 1980s and '90s disappeared with the application of superconductive transmission technology to the then-existent cable television systems."

BETWEEN THIS SHIT AND MY DAY JOB, IT'S LUCKY I FIND TIME TO SLEEP.

THE CAUSE IS FAR MORE IMPORTANT THAN YOUR SLEEP.

YEAH-- THAT'S WHAT THEY *ALL* SAY.

"With systems offering 500, then 1000, and eventually *5000* channels, it became economically infeasible for advertisers to support mainstream dramatic programming. Soon, instead of hundreds of thousands of viewers, audience shares were calculated in the *tens*."

"With the dissolution of the FCC, cable access was open to all persuasions. In a resurgence similar to that seen during the mid-1980s, religious programming became a television staple, outnumbering non-doctrinal programs nearly 100 to 1."

JEEZ-- THIS THING'S AN *ANTIQUE.* IT MUST WEIGH TWO OR THREE POUNDS!

BE CAREFUL. IT TOOK MONTHS TO LOCATE.

I'LL SET IT ON A MEDIUM SHOT, YOU AND THE BACKDROP. PRETTY DULL STUFF COMPARED TO THE SOUND MASSAGE AND SUBLIMINALS YOUR COMPETITION'S BEEN USING--

THE TRUTH OF MY MESSAGE WILL SHINE LIKE A BEACON. THE OTHERS ARE PRETENDERS--

I PREACH THE GOSPEL-- OF--

IT'S *YOUR* MONEY.
GET READY-- I SHOULD HAVE
YOU ON IN A COUPLE
OF MINUTES.

"With so many programs to choose from, viewer perceptions changed. Much as the fast-cut visual styles of the '90s were defined by 5, then 2 second commerci.ls, the style of mid-century programming was changed with the introduction of the retinal switch, or 'eye-box.'"

I KNOW THERE
ARE OTHERS WITH THE
VISION. OTHERS WHO HAVE
HEARD THE CALL THESE
PAST FEW MONTHS.

"The 'eye-box' was designed to detect minute changes in the capillaries of the retina, initiating random channel changes based on involuntary blood pressure fluctuations. To hold audiences, programmers were forced to devise new styles of programming that would not 'trip' the eye-box switcher."

--THE *TRUE*
MESSIAH--!

IT'S OKAY,
DOC. I HOOKED
UP A GUY LAST
WEEK WHO SAID
THE MESSIAH
WAS PLAYING
THIRD BASE FOR
THE OSAKA
PISTONS.

DOESN'T
MATTER TO
ME.

...GIMME
THAT OLD
TIME
RELIGION.

BUT
IF THAT
THING'S
GOD...

19

WHAT WAS THAT OLD SLOGAN? 'THE MARINES WANT A FEW GOOD MEN'. I REALLY BELIEVED THAT KIND OF SHIT WHEN I SIGNED ON. THAT WAS BEFORE ACHERON. BEFORE I CAME HOME.

"I HADN'T BEEN OFF BASE IN YEARS. IT DIDN'T TAKE LONG TO REMEMBER WHY."

LANCE CORPORAL HICKS TO SEE COLONEL STEPHENS.

OH--! I MEAN--I'M SORRY--THEY'RE EXPECTING YOU--

"I'D HEARD ABOUT STEPHENS-- SPECIAL PROJECTS MAN. HE HAD ZIP COMBAT EXPERIENCE, BUT FANCIED HIMSELF A REAL WARRIOR. EASY TO DO IN PEACETIME."

CORPORAL HICKS? I--I'M GLAD YOU COULD MAKE IT DOWN. AT EASE.

"HE KEPT HIS HANDS BEHIND HIS BACK. AFRAID TO TOUCH ME."

I TAKE IT YOU'VE SEEN THE DISC ON "THE DUTTON."

YESSIR.

THEN YOU KNOW--

YESSIR. YOU COULD SAY THAT.

I UNDERSTAND YOU HAVE SOME--EXPERIENCE-- IN THESE MATTERS.

DOCTOR, PLEASE--LET ME HANDLE THE--

WELL? IS IT TRUE?

22

"I WAS PART OF A DETATCHMENT SENT TO INVESTIGATE LOSS OF CONTACT WITH A TERRAFORMER COLONY ON THE PLANET ACHERON. COMMAND SUSPECTED AN ALIEN PRESENSE WAS INVOLVED.

"THE COLONY HAD BEEN RANSACKED. WE FOUND A SINGLE SURVIVOR--A YOUNG GIRL NAMED NEWT. THE REST OF THE COLONISTS WERE DEAD.

"BEFORE THE SQUAD COULD EFFECT DUST-OFF, WE WERE FORCED TO ENGAGE THE ALIEN ENEMY IN CLOSE QUARTERS.

"OTHER THAN MYSELF, A CIVILIAN NAMED RIPLEY, AND THE YOUNG GIRL, NO ONE FROM THE MISSION SURVIVED."

SURVIVAL IS SUCH A *RELATIVE* TERM, CORPORAL HICKS. I'VE BEEN READING YOUR FILE.

YOU HAD A STERLING RECORD PRIOR TO THE ACHERON MISSION.

SINCE YOUR RELEASE FROM MEDICAL THIS SEEMS TO HAVE-- CHANGED.

SIR, I WASN'T AWARE THAT *MY* RECORD WAS THE SUBJECT OF THIS DISCUSSION.

COLONEL, *PLEASE*, MAY I HAVE A FEW MOMENTS WITH THE CORPORAL-- *ALONE?*

MUCH BETTER. I FEEL STIFLED BY MILITARY IGNORANCE, DON'T YOU?

LOOK, WHATEVER YOUR NAME IS--YOU WANT TO TALK ABOUT THOSE ALIEN BASTARDS, FINE--

--BUT I DON'T SEE HOW MY *RECORD* IS PERTINENT TO--

MY NAME IS ORONA--AND IT'S *ENTIRELY* PERTINENT. PERHAPS A *REVIEW* IS IN ORDER.

"IN THE COURSE OF YOUR MISSION TO ACHERON YOU SUFFERED SEVERE ACID BURNS -- DEEP AND QUITE DISFIGURING."

GAAAGGHH--!

"ONCE BACK ON EARTH, YOU SPENT SEVERAL MONTHS IN QUARANTINE WAITING TO BE CLEARED INTO THE GENERAL POPULACE. THERE WAS CONSIDERABLE CONCERN OVER THE-- *INFECTIOUS* NATURE OF THE ALIEN SPORE.

"ACCORDING TO HOSPITAL REPORTS, YOU DIDN'T HAVE A SINGLE VISITOR DURING THIS ENTIRE PERIOD."

24

"WHEN YOU WERE FINALLY REINSTATED TO ACTIVE DUTY, THERE SEEM TO HAVE BEEN PROBLEMS IN--*READJUSTING*-- TO MILITARY LIFE. FORMER COMRADES, FEARFUL YOU MIGHT SOMEHOW BE 'INFECTIOUS' FROM THE ALIEN BLOOD, AVOIDED CONTACT.

"YOUR LATER RECORD IS PAINFULLY REPETITIVE--DRUNK AND DISORDERLY, BRAWLING, PUBLIC INTOXICATION. REALLY QUITE DISAPPOINTING."

OH GOD NO-- DON'T TOUCH ME! DON'T TOUCH ME!

I'M A GENETICIST, CORPORAL, BUT IT DOESN'T REQUIRE A PSYCHOLOGIST TO SEE A PATTERN IN THIS SELF-DESTRUCTIVE BEHAVIOR.

ALL OF IT STEMMING FROM THE ACHERON MISSION.

WHAT THE HELL DO YOU WANT FROM ME?

BEFORE THOSE COAST GUARD FOOLS DESTROYED THEMSELVES, THEY MANAGED TO TRANSMIT THE DATA BANKS FROM THE DERELICT TO OUR GROUND STATION.

WE HAVE THE ENTIRE INBOARD HISTORY, INCLUDING COURSE TRAJECTORIES.

CLICK

YOU SEEK REDEMPTION. I SEEK--

SPECIMENS.

25

SHE'S DREAMING AGAIN. WHAT DID YOU GIVE HER?

IT DOESN'T MAKE SENSE. THE DREAMS ARE GETTING *WORSE*.

WE MAY HAVE TO UP THE DOSAGE.

STANDARD THERAPY-- 30 MGS OF TRINOMINE.

IS THAT WISE? MUCH HIGHER AND YOU RUN THE RISK OF PERMANENT BRAIN DAMAGE.

IT'S A TRADE-OFF. ISN'T IT?

WHA--?!

NEWT! WAKE UP! YOU HAVE A VISITOR.

27

28

Excerpts from the confidential paper "Theory of Alien Propagation" by Dr. Waidslaw Orona, civilian advisor to the Colonial Marine Corps.

Humans suffer from peculiarly self-centered notions as to the nature of life. We assume out of hand that other lifeforms must somehow *conform* to our comfortable standards of logic and morality. This, of course, is absurd.

Our human "morality" is a thin tissue of arbitrary principle, easily ignored when expedient. Why should we expect more from alien lifeforms than we expect from *ourselves*?

As a matter of practical fact, much of what we presume to know about the alien lifeform is conjecture. However, amidst the theory, there are two absolute, unequivocal facts:

1) They are not like us.

2) We will *never* truly understand them.

29

Judging from the alien's dense exoskeleton and remarkable adaptability, we must assume their homeworld to be a harsh, desolate environment.

We know from the encounter on Acheron that the aliens have a Queen-based hierarchy. We also know they form hives to protect their young.

At some point, perhaps cyclical, the hive's queen must sense the instinctive need to propagate new colonies, and lays eggs that will later hatch as queen-larvae.

At the proper time, the drones provide host bodies for the fledgling queens.

For many in the research community, this parasitical breeding process is the single most disturbing aspect of the entire alien phenomenon.

Given the aliens' legendary "temperament," it's likely that these special breeding eggs are quickly removed from the queen's chamber and sheltered elsewhere.

Of course, for the aliens, it is completely natural—their equivalent of giving a bottle to a baby.

The actual incubation period is relatively short, a matter of days or even hours.

Birth is an ordeal of pain and violence.

As the fledgling queens emerge, there may well be a battle for dominance. Imagine a species where the first conscious act of life is *killing*.

Even so, I hesitate to imply any sort of "Darwinian" connotation to these struggles.

Killing may merely be a way for the newborn queen to define its own reality.

Soon, the new queen would lead a contingent of drones away from the old hive.

The drones are the queen's slaves, and there would be nothing more important than the construction of the new hive.

If natural building material were unavailable, perhaps other—*elements*—would be substituted.

One would not describe this as cannibalism so much as a remarkably ruthless *practicality*.

The nesting instinct is a powerful one. Early on, all effort would be concentrated on completing the hive.

The aliens would not think in terms of sacrifice. The hive is all. To assume death has *meaning* to these creatures is to deny their *greatest* power.

All ecosystems exist in a delicate state of balance. This would be as true of the alien homeworld as our own.

At home, the aliens would have any number of natural enemies.

Some would live, some would die, and the alien herd would be kept in check.

The bodies of the dead would be used to reinforce the walls of the hive. The cycle would continue. The ecosystem would survive.

The violent, uncontrollable alien infestations occurred when the creatures were *removed* from their natural habitat.

We can only guess how this might have happened. Perhaps it was millions of years ago. Perhaps only decades.

The end result is all that matters. Somehow the aliens were transplanted to other worlds.

The creatures would not be concerned with the particulars of their environment. They would concern themselves only with *circumstances*.

The natural predators were gone. The balance was gone.

All that was left was *prey*.

We humans believe our technology has made us invincible—that we've evolved *beyond* the simple notion of predator and prey.

Certainly there was no reason for the crews of the *Nostromo* or the *Sulaco*, or the settlers on Acheron to believe otherwise.

Man has never been comfortable in space. Even with our ships and atmosphere suits and weapons, we are intruders.

A hostile environment—ample quarry—the aliens must have felt *utterly* at home.

Humans have confused comfort with survival. For us mere *existence* isn't enough. We demand the *accoutrements* of life as well.

The aliens make no such demands. They live in a very simple world.

They live to kill.

They live to breed.

And finally, they *survive*.

37

"I'M STARING AT THE CEILING. TRANKED AGAIN-- THORADIN. I THINK. THE ONE THAT MAKES YOU FEEL LIKE YOU'RE SUFFOCATING.

"I RELIVE THE PAST AGAIN AND AGAIN. I WAS BORN ON A TERRAFORMER TRANSPORT IN DEEP SPACE. MY PARENTS NAMED ME REBECCA, BUT EVERYONE CALLED ME NEWT.

"OUR NEW HOME WAS A DESOLATE ROCK CHRISTENED ACHERON. MY PARENTS HAD VOLUNTEERED FOR THE MISSION IN THE ROMANTIC SPIRIT OF THE OLD EARTH PIONEERS, BUT THERE WAS LITTLE ROMANCE ON THAT CRUEL WORLD.

"THE WIND AND THE COLD MEANT NOTHING TO THE ALIENS. THEY WAITED, DORMANT, UNTIL THE TIME WAS RIGHT. I WAS THE ONLY SURVIVOR."

"I WAS FOUND BY A MARINE RESCUE TEAM AND RETURNED TO EARTH. THE DOCTORS LOST INTEREST IN ME WHEN I DIDN'T RESPOND TO THEIR TREATMENTS.

"I'M STARING AT THE CEILING. THERE'S A CIRCULAR LIGHT IN THE CENTER, HUMMING SOFTLY.

"CRACKS SPREAD ACROSS THE PLASTER, LIKE WRINKLES ON A OLD MAN'S FACE-- NO. LIKE THE WRINKLES ON *MY* FACE.

"SOME SEE SPACE AS A PANACEA-- UNCOUNTED WORLDS WITH UNTOLD RICHES. THEY LOOK TO THE HEAVENS AND SEE THE JOY OF OPPORTUNITY.

"I LOOK INTO SPACE AND SEE THE COLD VOID OF HELL. MY ONLY ESCAPE."

HICKS! DON'T LEAVE ME!

I UNDERSTAND YOU THINK HICKS MAY BE A PROBLEM.

MAY BE? HELL, THE MAN'S BEEN BUCKING FOR A PSYCH DISCHARGE EVER SINCE HE CAME BACK FROM ACHERON.

LOOKS LIKE YOU'VE GOT A PROBLEM, STEPHENS. COMMAND'S SOLD ON THE GUY.

YEAH--THEY THINK HE'S THE BIG TOUGH MONSTER KILLER. CREW KILLER IS MORE LIKE IT.

IT'S NOT LIKE THE ACHERON MISSION WAS A SUCCESS. HELL, THE ONLY SURVIVORS WERE A KID, A CIVILIAN NAMED RIPLEY AND HICKS.

THE KID'S A BRAIN CASE AND RIPLEY-- WELL YOU KNOW WHAT BECAME OF HER.

WHICH MEANS HICKS IS THE ONLY EXPERIENCED HAND AVAILABLE.

COMMAND'S MOVED HIM IN WITH THE GRUNTS AND HE'S SUPERVISING LOADING OPERATIONS.

I DON'T NEED HIS KIND OF EXPERIENCE. C'MON, BILL, YOU'VE STILL GOT SOME PULL OVER AT--

WHAT THE HELL IS THIS, STEPHENS? YOU DON'T LIKE HICKS? CROSS HIM OFF YOUR PARTY LIST. BUT HE'S GOT THE EXPERIENCE AND HE'S GOT THE MISSION. UNDERSTOOD?

YESSIR. UNDERSTOOD.

43

ANY OTHER NEWS ON THAT MERGER PROPOSAL WE SENT OVER WITH MASSEY?

I THOUGHT I TOLD YOU. THEY WENT FOR IT.

SWAK!

GOTCHA!

WENT FOR IT?

YEAH. LOWER PRICE PER SHARE, TOO. I GUESS MASSEY CONVINCED THEM OUR OFFER WAS GOOD BUSINESS.

WOCK!

GOOD MATCH.

YEAH. I ALMOST WORKED UP A SWEAT.

LISTEN, TED, I WANTED TO TALK TO YOU ABOUT THE BIOWARFARE PROJECT.

ANY MOVEMENT FROM THE GOVERNMENT?

YOU KNOW THOSE GOVERNMENT GUYS. HUSH-HUSH, BIG SECRET.

THEY WANT TO GRAB THE LIFEFORM PATENT FOR THEMSELVES.

CAN'T HAVE THAT.

ALIEN LIFEFORMS ARE THE NEXT STEP IN COMPETITIVE BIOLOGICAL WEAPONRY.

WE'VE ALREADY GOT INTEREST FROM CANADA, JAPAN, IRELAND--AND THE THIRD WORLD'S GOING APE.

PAT-- COFFEE'LL BE READY IN A MINUTE.

I WANT SOMEONE SPECIAL TO LOOK AFTER OUR INTERESTS. MASSEY DID A GOOD JOB ON THE MERGER. TELL ME ABOUT HIM.

DADDY--WHY DO THEY CALL IT 'THE WALL STREET JOURNAL'?

MBA FROM HARVARD, DOCTORATE IN LAW FROM CORNELL-- HE COULD HAVE HAD HIS PICK OF THE BIG TWO COMPANIES.

HONEY-- DON'T BE LATE!

INSTEAD HE ENLISTED IN THE *MARINES*, FOR CHRIST'S SAKE.

SILVER STAR FOR BRAVERY DURING THE OIL WAR. COUPLE HUNDRED CONFIRMED KILLS--

GOOD MORNING, MISTER MASSEY!!

HE DIDN'T ENLIST OUT OF PATRIOTISM. HE *LIKED* IT.

HE HAD MORE DECORATIONS THAN A CHRISTMAS TREE, THEN SUDDENLY, HE WAS COURT MARTIALED.

SEEMS HE TRIED TO KILL HIS COMMANDING OFFICER FOR FAILING TO ORDER HIS SQUAD TO ATTACK A CIVILIAN ENCAMPMENT.

WE PAID OFF THE MILITARY TRIBUNAL IMMEDIATELY. IT'S RARE WHEN YOU FIND A MAN WHO LOVES HIS WORK.

45

THE DARKNESS IS A BLANKET.

SOMETHING DRIPS LIKE SWEAT, ALL WARM AND STICKY.

IT FEELS GOOD.

WE WERE ONE. GOD, I LOVED YOU.

FLY, FLY AWAY, MY BRAVE LITTLE CAPTAIN--

THEN I WAS TORN FROM YOU, FORCED INTO THIS NAKED EXISTENCE, SO ALONE AND COLD. I NEVER THOUGHT I'D FEEL THAT LOVE AGAIN.

MY TRUE MOTHER IS PART OF ME. I CAN FEEL HER, SLIDING WET IN MY THROAT, FILLING MY LUNGS AND MY STOMACH, WRAPPING HER FINGERS INSIDE SO WARM, SO WARM--

HER TEETH GLITTER LIKE THE STARS. GOD. SHE IS IMPOSSIBLY BEAUTIFUL.

SHE LOVES ME MORE THAN YOU EVER COULD.

47

48

49

51

"NEWT'S ROOM WAS ON THE FORTIETH FLOOR OF THE MEDICAL HIGHRISE. EVEN WITH THE AUTOMATIC SECURITY SYSTEM BLINKED, THEY'D HAVE THE GROUND EXITS COVERED BY NOW."

DAMN, KID, YOU LOOK LIKE SHIT.

LOOK... WHO'S TALKING... *CUF* *CUF*...

WHA-- WHAT ARE YOU DOING--?

A LITTLE REMODELING, MARINE STYLE.

POOM!

KEEP YOUR HEAD DOWN! WE GO IN EIGHT!

POOM!

POOM! POOM!

HOLD TIGHT!

"THE WALL BLEW OUT FROM THE FORCE OF THE EXPLOSION AND WE WENT ALONG WITH IT. NICE VIEW.

BOOM!

"THE JET RESCUE TECHNOLOGY HAD BEEN DEVELOPED AFTER THE WORLD TRADE CENTER SMOKED IN '24. I'D 'BORROWED' THE SHIP AND THE HANDHELD CONTROLLER FROM CIVILIAN OPERATIONS.

CAUTION: POWERFUL DRAFT

"THE SHIP HAD BEEN DESIGNED FOR HIGH-RISE FIRE RESCUE, BUT I REMEMBER WHAT SERGEANT APONE USED TO SAY: 'MARINES DON'T QUIT. THEY ADAPT.'

"BY THE TIME THEY TRACED US BACK TO BASE IT WOULD BE TOO LATE.

"ONE OF THE JOYS OF TAKING A SUICIDE MISSION, I SUPPOSE--REPRIMANDS AND COURT-MARTIALS LOSE THEIR STING.

"I FLIPPED OFF THE REMOTE AND WE WERE MACH 2 BEFORE THE LAST PIECE OF PLASTER HIT GROUND LEVEL."

"FOR YEARS, THE GENERAL PUBLIC HAD BEEN FED THIS IMAGE OF MARINES AS 'INTELLECTUAL WARRIORS'--COLLEGE DIPLOMA IN ONE HAND, M-90 RAPID FIRE IN THE OTHER.

"I GUESS IT'S MORE COMFORTING TO IMAGINE THE NATIONAL DEFENSE SYSTEM IN THE HANDS OF A STIFF-EYED, EMOTIONLESS MARTINET THAN SOME SCARED TEENAGER WITH A SKIN PROBLEM."

CORPORAL HICKS! IS THERE SOMETHING WRONG?

YEAH, THE DODGERS ARE STILL IN LOS ANGELES. AT EASE, SON.

"AFTER A WHILE, THE MARINES THEMSELVES BOUGHT THE MYTH. BIG MISTAKE. SOLDIERS HAVE THE SAME WANTS AND DESIRES AS EVERYONE ELSE. SOMETIMES THEY DO THINGS NOT BECAUSE IT'S RIGHT OR WRONG, BUT BECAUSE THEY MUST."

WE'RE GOING BACK, AREN'T WE? WE'RE REALLY GOING BACK!

"FOR INSTANCE, NOBODY EXPECTS A MARINE CORPORAL TO SMUGGLE AN UNAUTHORIZED PASSENGER ABOARD A TOP SECURITY MILITARY FLIGHT."

"MAYBE THAT'S WHY IT WAS SO DAMN EASY."

"STEPHENS WAS GOING TO BE TROUBLE.

"PULLING THOSE PLASMA WEAPONS TO TEACH ME A LESSON IN MILITARY PROTOCOL WAS STUPID.

"WAIT UNTIL HE FINDS NEWT TUCKED AWAY IN THE AFT COMPARTMENT.

"STILL, I FELT SORRY FOR HIM, JUST LIKE I FELT SORRY FOR THE GRUNTS.

"I WAS TAKING THEM INTO MY WAR AND THEY DIDN'T EVEN KNOW IT.

"THE FORCE OF THE LIFT-OFF CRUSHED ANY LAST DOUBTS. I WAS BACK IN SPACE. AND NOTHING WAS GOING TO STOP ME."

GREAT SHOW! I HAVEN'T HEARD INDUSTRIAL NOISE LIKE THAT SINCE COLLEGE!

WE DESERVE A LITTLE REC TIME. IT'S BEEN HELL AND A HALF SINCE WE STARTED PLANNING THE INTERCEPT MISSION.

1990'S HOLOGRAM SHOW

DAVID BYRNE

LAURIE ANDE

EINSTUERZENDE NEUBAUTEN

199

LAURIE A DAVID BYR

TICKETS

ADMISSION
ADULT 100
CHILD 50

RIGHT NOW EVERYTHING LOOKS GOOD, BUT I'M STILL A LITTLE WORRIED ABOUT THAT LAST MINUTE BUSINESS WITH MASSEY.

IT WAS A DAMNED STUPID MISTAKE.

APPARENTLY ONE OF THE COMMUNICATIONS PEOPLE SENT MASSEY SOME CLASSIFIED MAIL THROUGH AN UNCLASSIFIED CHANNEL.

UNFORTUNATELY, MASSEY'S SON ACCESSED THE MATERIAL.

TOP SECRET

EYES ONLY

HEY, MOM! LOOK AT THIS!

OK MY GOD.

VERY CARELESS.

INFORMATION'S SKETCHY AT THIS POINT, BUT MASSEY'S WIFE APPEARS TO HAVE CONFRONTED HIM ABOUT THE DOCUMENT.

PAT--WE JUST SAW THIS HORRIBLE--*THING*-- ON THE READ SCREEN--

TAKE IT EASY, MISTER MASSEY. WE'LL BE DONE SOON.

REGULATIONS ARE QUITE CLEAR ON PROCEDURE IN CASES LIKE THIS, BUT YOU MUST ADMIT IT WAS AN UNUSUAL SIT- UATION. HE'D BEEN MARRIED CLOSE TO SIX YEARS.

HE TOOK PAINS TO MAKE IT LOOK LIKE A ROBBERY GONE BAD. THE POLICE DIDN'T SUSPECT A THING.

UNDER THE CIRCUMSTANCES, MASSEY PERFORMED ADMIRABLY. I HAD THE PSYCH BOYS DO A WORKUP ON HIM RIGHT BEFORE LIFTOFF AND HE REGISTERED WELL WITHIN TOLERABLE LIMITS.

I WONDER HOW IT FEELS-- BEING A SOCIOPATH I MEAN.

I WOULD IMAGINE IT'S QUITE *LIBERATING.*

BIONATIONAL
INTERNAL
MEMORANDUM

OPERATION:
OUTREACH

Progress report. The Government vessel *Benedict* launched on schedule 4/5/54. First in command, Col. Stephens, second in command, Cpl. Hicks.

Our chase ship *K-014* launched in pursuit immediately thereafter, captained by Bionational Executive Assistant Patrick Massey.

The government is seeking to retrieve specimens of an alien lifeform for its Weapons Development Program. If they are successful, this could seriously impact Bionational's claim of sole patent right on the new lifeform technology.

The *K-014*'s mission is twofold. First, to follow the *Benedict* to the alien homeworld and gather biological data on the lifeform.

Second, to inhibit the *Benedict*'s crew from retrieving a viable test subject. Captain Massey has been given *carte blanche* toward this end.

In the interim, our Bionational research team continues its examination of the human specimen salvaged from the ejected pilot's pod of the cargo vessel *Junket*.

SOMEONE'S OUT THERE, MOTHER.

CARGO EXPRESS
IDENTIFICATION

VALID FOR TYPE 5

225·7083·1
NON·TRANSFERABLE

JAMES LIKOWSKI···SECTION 10-B611
PILOT···CLASSIFICATION 2-S

Human specimen's pod had been damaged, causing loss of atmosphere, but vital signs were somehow *preserved* by the infusion of the alien lifeform.

After retrieval, both specimen's were brought to Bionational's Houston labs for analysis.

SOMETHING TOUCHES ME, MOTHER. I CAN FEEL IT IN MY ARMS, MY CHEST--

Preliminary reports from our weapons specialists are encouraging. Full-scale testing should commence within the next 48 hours. We shall provide daily updates for all members of the Bionational board.

PROTECT ME, MOTHER. DON'T LET THEM HURT ME--

--PLEASE.

Dr. Ranier: Start wherever you'd like.

Patient Heerman: Okay. Okay. **(pause)** I'm with my mother. We're still in L.A. —

Dr. Ranier: Your mother died several years ago?

Patient Heerman: Cancer. **(pause)** We're taking the Wilshire tube into downtown L.A. Right then I knew I was dreaming...I've *never* seen an empty tube.

Patient Heerman: All of the sudden, we hear this loud—*scraping* sound —

Dr. Ranier: Scraping? How do you mean?

Patient Heerman: Like...like fingernails ripping fabric. **(pause)** Then, suddenly, the car *stops* —

Patient Heerman: Something was trying to...*get in.* I pounded on the door, hoping someone would hear us—

Patient Heerman: Then these—*things* started to—*claw* into the car. I ran to my mother and she made this sick, *bubbling* sound, deep in her chest—

Patient Heerman: It was just a stupid nightmare, right? *Right?*

Dr. Morgan: What happened after the television came on?

Patient Culp: First, there was only distortion—but then something started to —

Patient Culp: — *come* at me, from *inside* the screen —

Patient Duncan: I must have dosed off. The next thing I knew, the stewardess was standing next to me. I remember thinking that she reminded me of someone...

Dr. Frankel: Who?

Patient Duncan: (pause) It's going to sound funny, but—my mother.

Patient Duncan: All at once, these teeth—they...*it* ripped right through her chest—like it had been inside her the *whole time* —

Patient Lockwood: I kept screaming for my Mommy, but she wasn't there. Just the monster—coming *closer* and *closer* —

Patient Lockwood: It was shiny and wet and I think it wanted to kill me —

End transcript. Copy 2.3a2, Dr. Waidslaw Orona, Civilian Advisor, C.M.C.

FASCINATING ALL THESE REPORTS ARE FROM WITHIN A FIFTY MILE RADIUS.

YES, DOCTOR ORONA. AND I'VE GOT A DOZEN MORE JUST THE SAME. EVERY PATIENT RATES 'SENSITIVE' ON THE CRYER SCALE AND DOUBLE FIGURES ON THE EMERSON--

THE DESCRIPTIONS OF THE CREATURES-- THEY'RE CONSISTANT?

IDENTICAL.

SOME OF THE TECHNICIANS ON THE PSYCH SIDE DID A WORK UP POSTULATING DIFFERENT MODES OF COMMUNICATION FOR THE ALIEN CREATURES.

THE MOST PLAUSIBLE WAS TELEPATHY--OR AT LEAST SOME *FORM* OF TELEPATHY.

YOU THINK THEY'RE TRYING TO COMMUNICATE WITH US?

UNLIKELY. THE THE DATA WE'VE COLLECTED DOESN'T SUGGEST HIGHER INTELLIGENCE.

THE 'SIGHTINGS' ARE RANDOM AND CONFINED TO A SPECIFIC GEOGRAPHIC AREA--VERY ODD.

WE'VE KEPT THE EXISTANCE OF THE ALIEN CREATURES COMPLETELY SECRET. ALL OF A SUDDEN WE ARE EXPERIENCING A *WAVE* OF SPONTANEOUS TELEPATHIC EVENTS.

THE QUESTION IS, WHY NOW? AND WHY *EARTH*?

63

"MOTHER! WHERE ARE YOU?"

"OH JESUS. IT HURTS ALL OVER. I'M SCARED."

HE'S COMING OUT OF IT.

BP IS SLIGHTLY ELEVATED; HEART RATE AND RESPIRATION NORMAL. I SHOW NO MOVEMENT FROM THE PARASITE. IT APPEARS DORMANT.

YOUR NAME IS JAMES LIKOWSKI, YOU WERE CAPTAIN OF THE SPACE FREIGHTER, JUNKET. YOU ARE ON EARTH IN A QUARANTINED MEDICAL FACILITY.

IF YOU'RE FEELING UP TO IT, WE'LL RELEASE YOU FROM THE STRAPS.

WHY AREN'T I DEAD?

64

I HAD LEVITZ DROP SOME HINTS AT THE SAN DIEGO ARMS FAIR AND *EVERYONE'S* EXCITED MAJOR QUAN'S BEGGING FOR A 60 DAY EXCLUSIVE.

QUAN CAN KISS MY ASS. WE'RE SETTING CONDITIONS, NOT THE CHINESE.

SO WHEN DOES BYNER THINK WE'LL HAVE SOMETHING TO SHOW?

COUPLE OF DAYS-- 72 HOURS, TOPS.

JESUS, YOU'VE BEEN STARING AT ME FOR HOURS. IS THAT ALL YOU WANT TO DO?

I'M SORRY. DOES IT BOTHER YOU?

NO-- I MEAN IT'S YOUR MONEY.

IT'S MY MONEY.

WOMEN ARE BLESSED. THEY KNOW HOW IT FEELS TO BE JOINED WITH ANOTHER LIFE-- --TO SHARE THEMSELVES SELFLESSLY. IT MUST BE WONDERFUL.

YEAH. WONDERFUL. MY BACK'S KILLING ME.

C'MON, BABE, YOU'RE MAKING ME FEEL WEIRD. ARE YOU SURE YOU DON'T WANT *SOMETHING?*

YES. I WANT TO KNOW HOW IT *FEELS.*

SALVAJE! WHERE THE HELL HAVE YOU BEEN?

STUDYING.

YEAH? WELL, STUDY THIS.

A COUPLE OF GOVERNMENT SUITS DROPPED BY THE SHOP TODAY. IT SEEMS THEY'RE REAL INTERESTED IN CHANNEL 2393.

WHAT DID YOU TELL THEM?

I DIDN'T TELL THEM SHIT. IF THEY KNEW I WAS HOOKING UP ILLEGALS THEY'D PULL MY LICENSE AND I'D LOSE ALL MY MILITARY CONTRACTS.

THEN EVERYTHING IS FINE.

NO, EVERYTHING IS NOT FINE.

LOOK, I'VE BEEN HOOKING UP YOU RELIGIOUS PSYCH JOBS FOR THREE YEARS NOW...

AND I'VE NEVER HAD PROBLEMS WITH THE FCC, COPS OR ANYBODY ELSE--

UNTIL NOW!

DAMN IT, SALVAJE-- WHAT THE HELL IS THAT THING?

HOW LONG UNTIL THE NEXT COMMUNICATION FROM THE BENEDICT?

ANOTHER HOUR. WE'RE ZEROED ON THEIR LOCAL ANTENNA. WE *SHOULD* BE ABLE TO GET A CLEAR TRANSMISSION.

GOOD. KEEP YOUR DISTANCE. THEY'RE LOADED WITH D.S. SENSORS--

--DON'T WANT THEM TO SPOT US UNTIL *AFTER* WE GO THROUGH GRAVITY BURN.

OKAY, ONE MORE TIME.

THE GOVERNMENT SHIP HAS FIVE BASIC ACCESS PORTS: TWO FORE, TWO AFT AND THE LOADING BAY.

WE'LL BE GOING IN THROUGH THE #1 AFT LOCK.

YOU'LL ALL HAVE LOW LEVEL BLASTERS. BE CAREFUL.

MILITARY SHIPS ARE ARMORED, BUT AN UNLUCKY SHOT COULD STILL RUPTURE THE HULL.

K-SHUNK

SAVE THE GUNS FOR *SOFT* TARGETS -- INTERNAL SYSTEMS, ELECTRONICS, CREW.

WE'LL HOLD THE CREW PRISONER UNTIL WE REACH THE ALIEN HOMEWORLD.

ONCE WE'RE THROUGH WE WILL PURGE THE MILITARY COMPUTERS AND DESTROY THE SHIP.

NO SURVIVORS OF COURSE.

"I PULLED NEWT OUT OF THE SPARE CARGO LOCK 12 HOURS AFTER LIFT OFF.

"IT LOOKED LIKE THE DRUGS WERE WEARING OFF THOUGH IT WAS HARD TO TELL.

"I FELT SORRY FOR HER.

"STEPHENS TOOK IT ABOUT AS WELL AS EXPECTED."

I TOLD THE BASE COMMANDER YOU WERE UNRELIABLE, HICKS BUT THIS--THIS IS INSANITY!

WHAT THE HELL WERE YOU THINKING? DID YOU 'THINK' AT ALL?

I OFFER NO EXCUSES SIR. I DID WHAT--

NO EXCUSES! OH, THAT'S VERY MANLY. MAYBE YOU COULD TRY AN EXPLANATION--IF NOT FOR ME, THEN FOR THE MEN.

EXPLAIN WHY YOU BROUGHT EXTRA WEIGHT ONTO A CAREFULLY BALANCED GRAVITY DRIVE SHIP--

70

IT'S NOT HIS FAULT--HE DID IT FOR ME--

OH, I UNDERSTAND NOW!

IT'S NOT HIS FAULT! YOU FORCED HIM TO STOW YOU ABOARD!

FORCED HIM TO JEOPARDIZE THE MISSION!

LEAVE HER OUT OF IT. IT'S MY RESPONSIBILITY. AND THE GRAVITY BALANCE IS NOMINAL.

I DUMPED 104 POUNDS OF THAT RASBERRY FLAVORED SHIT FROM THE SHIPS STORES JUST BEFORE WE TOOK OFF.

SHUT UP, EISLEY.

I LIKED THAT RASBERRY FLAVORED SHIT.

I SHOULD LOCK YOUR ASS UP AND KEEP YOU THERE UNTIL THE COURT MARTIAL.

I'M SURE THE MILITARY COURT WOULD BE INTERESTED IN HEARING HOW A TOP SECRET MILITARY VESSEL LEFT BASE...

WITHOUT A THOROUGH INSPECTION BY THE COMMANDING OFFICER, SIR.

BUT THE MISSION COMES AHEAD OF MY PERSONAL DESIRES, OKAY--

THE GIRL IS YOUR RESPONSIBILITY, HICKS. WE'LL SETTLE THE REST WHEN WE RETURN TO EARTH

IF WE RETURN TO EARTH.

MAN, I'VE NEVER SEEN STEPHENS SO *PISSED.*

I THINK THERE'S SOMETHING *SERIOUSLY* WRONG WITH OUR CORPORAL HICKS. BUT WHAT THE HELL--THE GIRL'S CUTE.

BENSON, YOU IN?

NAW, I'VE GOT WALK-THROUGH. KEEP MY SEAT WARM.

THIS IS BENSON. I'M IN SECTION A FOR APPLE 5. NO VISIBLE HULL STRESS. PROCEEDING INTO A FOR APPLE 6.

BENEDICT TO K-014 PREPARE FOR TRANSMISSION OF UPDATED TELEMETRY DATA--

WHAT THE HELL?

OUR ETA WITH THE HOMEWORLD IS--

WHAT THE HELL IS *THIS?*

DO THE OTHERS KNOW--

SHHUNK!

ERGGG--

72

74

76

THE GUARDS ARE DEAD. I WANT TO KILL *MORE*. I CAN HEAR ALARMS. DON'T CARE.

FOOM!

FOOM!

FOOM!

CAN'T CARE.

GOT TO GET OUTSIDE. I WANT TO *FEEL* THE SUN.

POW! POW!

URGGHHH!

HOT OUTSIDE. WET WITH HUMIDITY.

GET OUT OF THE CAR!

MHZ UNLOADING ZONE

OH MY GOD--!

LEATHER SEATS--SMOOTH, SOFT-- I SMELL HOT OZONE AS I ACCELERATE.

SPAK

SPAK

SPAK

DEATH IS ALL AROUND ME.

KA HUMP

I FEEL UTTERLY ALIVE.

THE EXPRESSWAY CUTS DIRECTLY THROUGH THE CITY. I AM THINKING OF MY WIFE.

THEY TRY TO STOP ME BUT IT ISN'T POSSIBLE.

THEY DON'T UNDERSTAND. THIS IS *MY* TIME. I *CANNOT* BE DENIED.

I SEE ORANGE FLAMES. THERE IS A BURST OF HEAT. I *WANT* THEM TO SUFFER.

THE BUILDING IS AN OLD FRIEND. REAL FLOWERS OUT FRONT. THEY SMELL LIKE EXPENSIVE PERFUME.

I ENTER THE ELEVATOR. THE BUTTONS ARE SMOOTH, COOL PLASTIC. THE BURNISHED METAL PLATE GLOWS IN THE DIM GREEN LIGHT.

SO CLOSE. I ACHE FOR HER TOUCH.

WE TOUCH. FOR THE FIRST TIME IN MY LIFE, I UNDERSTAND PERFECTION.

GET HIM!

BAM BAM

JAMES?

82

83

YOUR NAME IS MARIS. UNDER THE PROVISIONS OF THE BAINES AMENDMENT YOU'VE BEEN DECLARED A *TERRORIST.*

YOU HAVE *NO RIGHTS* UNDER AMERICAN LAW. ANY MEANS MAY BE USED TO ELICIT INFORMATION, UP TO AND INCLUDING *PHYSICAL TORTURE.*

I--I CAN'T *FEEL* ANYTHING.

SPINAL BLOCKS. WE'VE DEADENED EVERYTHING FROM THE *NECK DOWN.*

DON'T WORRY. IT'S NOT *PERMANENT.* YET.

LET'S MAKE IT *SIMPLE.* TELL US ABOUT THE *CHURCH.* TELL US THEIR PLANS FOR THE *CREATURES.*

IF THEY FIND OUT I'VE TOLD YOU--

--THEY'LL MAKE ME ONE OF THEM--

I'M TOLD YOU'RE A *VIDEO TECHNICIAN--* GOOD WITH YOUR HANDS. THAT'S WHY I'M GOING TO START WITH YOUR *LEGS*

WE USED TO DO THIS *WITHOUT* ANESTHESIA...

...BUT THERE WERE *TERRIBLE* COMPLICATIONS FROM THE SHOCK.

TOP SECRET/ GOVERNMENT SECURITY CLEARANCE REQUIRED

I DIDN'T BOTHER WITH EDITING, DOCTOR ORONA. I THOUGHT YOU'D WANT TO SEE IT IMMEDIATELY.

HOW LONG BEFORE HE TALKED?

ALMOST NINE HOURS. I WAS QUITE IMPRESSED.

¡KAK KAK! -- I CONFESS TO ALL MY CRIMES. I AM GUILTY. WHAT'S IT MATTER?

I'VE SEEN THE INCUBATION. I'VE SEEN SALVAJE'S GOD YOU CAN'T BEGIN TO UNDERSTAND IT'S POWER.

IT WOULD BE EASIER FOR YOU IF I WERE PART OF SALVAJE'S CONSPIRACY AT LEAST THEN YOU'D HAVE A REASON -- SOMEONE TO BLAME.

MARIS--WE JUST GOT A CORPORATE ON THE WORKLINK. ARE YOU AVAILABLE?

CORPORATE SCALE? I'LL MAKE TIME.

IT'S THE SHEER COINCIDENCE OF IT THAT TERRIFIES YOU.

THE REAL WORLD'S LIKE THAT. RANDOM. CHAOTIC. CASUAL.

MARIS, VIDEOLINK, WE HAD A CALL ABOUT SOME CRYSTAL SWITCHING PROBLEMS?

OH, YEAH. JUST A MINUTE.

VIDEOLINK'S HERE. SHOULD I SEND HIM DOWN?

I REMEMBER THINKING-- JUST ANOTHER JOB.

THE REGULAR TECH'S OUT SICK-- ONE OF THOSE MUTATED FLU VIRUSES--

YOU DO MUCH CRYSTAL WORK?

NOT RECENTLY-- CORPORATE DESIGNATES HAVE A LOCK ON THE BEST JOBS.

WHEN YOU'RE FREELANCE IT'S ALMOST ALL PRIVATE OR MILITARY.

ROUTINE.

SWITCHER'S IN THE BACK. ANY QUESTIONS-- BEEP ME--

OTHERWISE I'LL CHECK BACK IN A HALF HOUR OR SO--

THANKS.

ONE OF THE LOGIC CHIPS HAD CRUNCHED. I HAD IT OUT IN UNDER A MINUTE.

I WAS--GOOD WITH MY HANDS.

THAT'S WHEN I SAW THEM. CHEAP LEAD SHUNTS, HAND-SOLDERED INTO THE OPTICS LINE. ABOUT AS SOPHISTICATED AS AN OLD STYLE FUSE.

SECURITY TYPES LIKE THEM BECAUSE THEY'RE PHYSICAL AND TEMPORARY. OF COURSE, THAT MAKES THEM EASY TO CIRCUMVENT.

DON'T KNOW WHY I BURNED THEM. CURIOSITY, MAYBE THE CHALLENGE.

MY GOD.

THEY'RE REAL.

89

"YOU SEE THE CREATURE WE CAPTURED WAS A QUEEN--

"--AND THAT CHANGED THINGS."

IT'S BIRTHING PROCESS IS UTTERLY *PARTHENOGENIC*, WITH NONE OF THE PRIMITIVE *RITUAL* ASSOCIATED WITH SEXUAL REPRODUCTION.

THE *AUSTERITY* OF IT ALL IS QUITE *BREATHTAKING.*

"IT SEEMS TO LIVE FOR ONLY ONE PURPOSE-- TO *REPRODUCE.*

"WHAT'S A *QUEEN* WITHOUT HER *SUBJECTS?*

"THE MARKETING PEOPLE WANT US TO HOLD OFF ON FURTHER TESTING UNTIL THEY CAN PUT TOGETHER A *PROMOTIONAL* CAMPAIGN FOR THE NOVEMBER *WEA-TECH* CONFERENCE.

"EVEN WITH THE *SECRECY,* BIONATIONAL'S INVESTMENT RATING HAS *DOUBLED* ON THE INTERNATIONAL BOARDS.

"OUR *ORGANIC WEAPONS* PROGRAM IS GOING TO *REVOLUTIONIZE* THE INDUSTRY.

"I'M SO *HAPPY* FOR YOU--

"--FOR *US.*"

I WAS STANDING AT ONE OF THE VIEWPORTS, STARING INTO SPACE. THE LIGHT FROM THE STARS STRETCHED AROUND THE SHIP LIKE GLOWING WHITE NEON.

I WAS TRYING TO REMEMBER MY PARENTS. ALL I COULD REMEMBER WAS THE *BLOOD*.

IT--IT'S AN OPTICAL ILLUSION.

WHAT?

THE STARS-- GRAVITY DRIVE'S SO POWERFUL WE'RE *BENDING* THE LIGHT. YOU GET USED TO IT. BEATS THE HELL OUT OF HIBERNATION.

THE MARINES WERE WARY OF CAPTAIN STEPHENS IN THE AFTERMATH OF PRIVATE BENSON'S DEATH. STEPHENS INSISTED IT WAS AN ACCIDENT, CLOSING THE INVESTIGATION BEFORE IT STARTED?

I COULD UNDERSTAND THAT ATTITUDE FROM STEPHENS. BUT WHAT ABOUT *HICKS*?

HELLO AGAIN. MIND IF I SIT HERE?

NO-- I MEAN IT'S ALRIGHT.

IN THE MIDST OF THIS, WHAT DID BUTLER SEE IN *ME*?

CORPORAL HICKS MUST THINK A LOT OF YOU TO STOW YOU ON BOARD.

STEPHENS IS GOING TO HAVE HIS *ASS* ONCE WE'RE BACK ON EARTH.

HICKS AND I--*UNDERSTAND* EACH OTHER.

YEAH-- I'LL BET YOU UNDERSTAND EACH OTHER *REAL* WELL--

KNOCK IT OFF, EASLEY.

COULDN'T HE FIND SOME- ONE HIS *OWN* AGE TO--

--I SAID *KNOCK* IT OFF!

92

93

HICKS GAVE ME A SCHEDULE OF TOKEN ADMINISTRATIVE DUTIES TO KEEP ME OCCUPIED DURING THE VOYAGE.

HATRED OF THE ALIENS BURNED INSIDE HIM LIKE AN OPEN FLAME. IT WAS ALL THAT SUSTAINED HIM.

PRIVATE BUTLER! DO YOU HAVE *BUSINESS* AT THIS STATION?

HE'D LOST ALL SENSE OF *COMPASSION.* HE SHRUGGED OFF BENSON'S DEATH AS IF IT WERE TRIVIAL-- AN *ANNOYANCE.*

I SHARED HIS HATRED OF THE ALIENS, BUT SUDDENLY OUR BITTER QUEST SEEMED EMPTY-- ALMOST *UGLY.*

HICKS-- HE WAS *ONLY*--

GET BACK WITH THE OTHERS, SOLDIER. *NOW!*

I *SAW* WHAT HE WAS *DOING!* IT'S GOING TO *STOP,* EVEN IF I HAVE TO CONFINE *BOTH* OF YOU TO YOUR QUARTERS.

WHAT'S *WRONG* WITH YOU? BUTLER WAS--

MY GOD. YOU'RE *JEALOUS.*

I'M NOT A *CHILD* ANYMORE. BUTLER'S MY FRIEND--

--MAYBE MY ONLY FRIEND. I WON'T LET YOU *RUIN* THAT.

94

95

:KAK KAK: --THE BIONATIONAL PEOPLE NEVER SUSPECTED. I REPLACED THE SHUNTS-- PRETENDED NOTHING HAD HAPPENED--

--ALL THE TIME KNOWING THAT I HAD TO FIND SALVAJE.

MARIS--GOT ANOTHER CALL FOR YOU. MAIN FEED'S GONE DOWN AT THE--

GET SOMEBODY ELSE.

OPEN UP, YOU CRAZY BASTARD! LET ME IN--!

POOM POOM POOM

WELCOME. I AM DIDI. WE ARE--

I KNOW WHO YOU ARE.

SALVAJE-- DAMN YOU, I'VE SEEN IT-- IT'S REAL!

SALVAJE'S VISION HAD TAPPED INTO SOMETHING PRIMAL, UNCONTROLLABLE. AS HIS MESSAGE SPREAD, THE DEVOTED SOUGHT HIM OUT--PROVIDED FOR HIM.

WELCOME BROTHER. PLEASE JOIN US IN OUR--

WHERE THE HELL IS HE?

97

98

THE CREATURE WATCHED PASSIVELY, HOVERING PROTECTIVELY OVER IT'S BROOD.

WE HAVE COME TO CONSUMMATE OUR LOVE--TO PURGE THE VISION FROM OUR MINDS--

--TO BE ONE WITH YOU.

TAKE ME. TAKE ME. TA--

IT BURST OUT IN A GLISTENING BLUR, VISCOUS TENDRILS OF FLUID FLUTTERING BEHIND IT LIKE SOME OBSCENE AFTERBIRTH.

I COULD SEE HIS MOUTH TWISTING IN PAIN AS THE CREATURE ATTACHED ITSELF--

--AND HE STARTED TO SCREAM.

--GGGAAAHHH--!

FOR THE FIRST TIME, SALVAJE UNDERSTOOD THE TRUE MEANING OF SACRIFICE.

--AAHHUKK!--

100

WHA--
MY GOD.
THEY'RE TAKING HER.

AGGH!

PLEASE-- TAKE ME-- PLEASE--!

UKGGU--!

THEY'RE TRYING TO DESTROY HER.

SIR--WE'RE UNDER SOME SORT OF ATTACK! I'VE LOST CONTACT WITH GROUND FLOOR SECURITY--

I THINK WE SHOULD NOTIFY THE--

NO OUTSIDERS! WE HANDLE THIS IN-HOUSE--

SALVAJE'S ACOLYTES DRAGGED THEIR INFECTED BRETHEREN OUTSIDE, MAKING ROOM FOR THE OTHERS. I SAW DOZENS TAKE THE SPORE.

THEY WERE ALL HER CHILDREN NOW.

KILLERS! MURDERERS!

THE QUEEN'S MINE!

BLAM BLAM
BLAM

I HEARD GUNFIRE OUTSIDE THE CHAMBER. SUDDENLY, THE ALIEN *SCREAMED.*

IT WAS THE CRY OF A *MOTHER* AT THE DEATH OF HER *CHILD.*

I BROKE AWAY FROM SALVAJE'S MEN AND STAGGERED BLINDLY THROUGH THE NEST.

THE LIFE FORM PATENTS BELONG *HERE.* WE DEVELOPED IT. WE NURTURED IT.

BLAM BLAM

BRAAAAAAP!

THERE'S TOO MANY OF THEM--WE CAN'T POSSIBLY--

--MOTHER OF--

102

KOFF KOFF--I DON'T REMEMBER MUCH AFTER THAT. SECURITY POLICE QUARANTINED THE BUILDING--THEY MUST HAVE FOUND ME INSIDE--

I JUST CAN'T UNDERSTAND. *WHY*-- WHY *ME*--?

OH MY GOD. IT MAKES *SENSE* NOW. SHE DID IT--THAT *THING*--

I'VE BEEN *PART* OF IT ALL ALONG. HOOKING UP *SALVAJE*, BURNING THE SECURITY STOPS--

KAK KAK--MAYBE IT GOES BACK EVEN *FURTHER*--BIRTH-- SCHOOL. *EVERY* DECISION OF MY LIFE--MAYBE SHE CONTROLLED IT *ALL*--

IT WASN'T *SALVAJE'S* CONSPIRACY--IT WAS *HERS*. I WAS JUST ANOTHER SOLDIER-- ANOTHER SACRIFICE--

OH GOD, PLEASE-- I'M *SCARED* OF DYING. I WANT TO *LIVE*. I WANT TO--

THAT'S *ENOUGH*. WHAT DID YOU DO WITH HIM?

ORGAN BANK'S TAKING WHAT THEY CAN USE-- EYES, SKIN, WHAT'S LEFT OF HIS STOMACH. THEY'LL BURN THE REST.

WE'RE WASTING TIME. WE STILL DON'T KNOW WHERE THE FANATICS ARE HIDING.

ACCORDING TO BIONATIONAL DOCUMENTATION ALIEN GESTATION TAKES ANYWHERE FROM 72 HOURS TO A WEEK OR MORE.

IF ANY OF THE NEWBORN *ESCAPE*--IF ANY OF THEM ARE *QUEENS*--

GOD HELP US ALL.

104

AS THE SHIP APPROACHED THE ALIEN'S HOMEWORLD, I WAS OVERWHELMED BY A HIDEOUS PREMONITION OF *DEATH*.

BUTLER AND I SPENT EVERY SPARE MOMENT TOGETHER. I KNEW HE *SHARED* MY APPREHENSIONS.

THERE WAS AN AIR OF *DESPERATION* TO OUR ENCOUNTERS AS IF WE DIDN'T DARE WASTE AN INSTANT.

WE MADE LOVE THAT FINAL DAY, SURROUNDED BY THE BLEAK GRAY METAL OF THE SHIP'S HULL.

AND FOR THE FIRST TIME SINCE ACHERON, I *CRIED*.

I REMEMBER THINKING HOW *FRAIL* WE WERE NEXT TO OUR MACHINES.

106

107

ANYBODY KNOW WHAT'S HAPPENING?

YOUR GUESS IS AS GOOD AS MINE. NOBODY CAN FIND STEPHENS OR HICKS.

WHAT ABOUT MEEKER?

SHE HAD COMMUNICATIONS DUTY. I HAVEN'T SEEN HER SINCE SHE--

SHIT! SOMEONE'S PULLED THE LOADER MECHANISM! THIS THING'S USELESS!

THIS ONE TOO.

THEY'VE ALL BEEN ZEROED. THIS IS SOME KIND OF SET-UP.

THIS IS CAPTAIN STEPHENS.

I WANT ALL CREW TO REPORT TO THE LOADING BAY-- IMMEDIATELY--

I SUPPOSE YOU'RE GOING TO KILL THE *REST* OF THEM--LIKE YOU KILLED *BENSON.*

WHAT HAPPENED-- HE CATCH YOU *TRANSMITTING* TO THESE BASTARDS?

GET OFF IT HICKS--

YOU DON'T CARE ABOUT THE DAMN "MARINES" ANY MORE THAN *I* DO. ALL YOU CARE ABOUT ARE YOUR PRECIOUS *ALIENS.*

THAT'S IT-- NICE AND EASY!

DOUBLE CHECK THE SHIP'S COMPLEMENT. MAKE SURE WE HAVE *EVERYONE.*

YOUR MARINES ARE *SAFE* FOR NOW, CORPORAL HICKS. WE STILL NEED AN ALIEN SPECIMEN-- AND THEY SEEM TO *THRIVE* ON HUMANS.

HUMANS? YOU THINK YOU CAN USE THE MARINES FOR *BAIT?* CHRIST, DIDN'T THEY--

THAT'S ENOUGH.

I DON'T *LIKE* YOU, STEPHENS. I DON'T MIND *GREEDY* MEN--

--BUT I CAN'T COUNTENANCE *TRAITORS*--EVEN WHEN THEY'RE ON *MY* SIDE. NEVER KNOW WHEN THEY MIGHT *TURN*--

WAIT-- MASSEY--YOU DON'T *UNDERSTAND*-- YOU *NEED* ME--

POOM!

NOT *ANYMORE.*

PREPARE THE DROPSHIP FOR LANDING.

WE'RE GOING *HUNTING.*

109

FOR ONE BRIEF MOMENT I'D FOUND LOVE. ONE OF HICK'S *GRUNTS*--A MARINE NAMED BUTLER--

I COULD FEEL THE PANIC RISING IN MY CHEST. CHOKING CLAUSTROPHOBIC.

THAT'S WHAT THE ENEMY *DEPENDS* ON. HUMAN-- ALIEN-- THEY RELY ON THAT FEAR TO *ENDURE.*

WHAT IS IT ABOUT LIFE THAT AS SOON AS YOU FIND SOMETHING *GOOD*-- IT'S TAKEN *AWAY* FROM YOU?

MY FIRST INSTINCT WAS TO *HIDE*--JUST LIKE ACHERON-- JUST LIKE EARTH.

NO!

THEY DON'T UNDERSTAND FEAR. THEY DON'T UNDERSTAND *ANYTHING* BEYOND THEIR OWN *EXISTENCE.*

IT EXPLAINED THE *RESILIENCE* OF CREATURES LIKE THE ALIEN.

I KNEW I WOULD HAVE TO BECOME *LIKE* THEM TO *SURVIVE.*

IT HAD BEEN FOUR HOURS SINCE WE'D BEEN BOARDED. WHO THE HELL *WERE* THEY? SOLDIERS? MERCENARIES?

THIS WAS EASIER THAN I'D *HOPED*. DID YOU DOUBLE-CHECK THE INBOARD ROSTER?

STEPHENS ACED BENSON AND MEEKER AND DUMPED THE BODIES BEFORE WE DOCKED--

THE REST OF THE COMPLEMENT IS ACCOUNTED FOR.

IT DIDN'T MATTER. IT WOULDN'T HAVE MATTERED TO *THEM.*

NO WONDER STEPHENS CHEWED MY ASS OVER PACKING PLASMA RIFLES. HE WAS AFRAID WE'D USE THEM AGAINST *YOU.*

I STILL CAN'T FIGURE WHERE THE CORPORATION FOUND THE *BALLS* TO INTERCEPT A GOVERNMENT SHIP ON A *CLASSIFIED* MISSION--

I THINK YOU'LL FIND THE CORPORATION CAPABLE OF ALMOST *ANYTHING.*

WE STILL BELIEVE IN FREE ENTERPRISE-- CAPITALISM. AND I'M AFRAID YOUR GOVERNMENT WANTS TO KEEP THE ALIEN LIFEFORM FOR *ITSELF.*

MY GOVERNMENT? YOU MAKE IT SOUND LIKE THE CORPORATION IS AN INDEPENDANT STATE--

JESUS, THOSE THINGS *DESTROYED* ACHERON. THINK WHAT THEY COULD DO ON *EARTH*--

I HAVE.

WE'RE *BREEDING* THEM.

111

YOU'LL STAY WITH ME ABOARD THE BENEDICT. YOUR MEN SEEM TO RESPECT YOU-- I MIGHT BE ABLE TO *USE* THAT--

YOU'VE ALREADY GOT THOSE THINGS ON EARTH--WHY NOT JUST *KILL* US AND BE DONE WITH IT?

OH, BUT YOU'RE *GOING* TO DIE--REST ASSURED OF THAT.

BUT I'M SURE YOU UNDERSTAND THE CALL OF SCIENCE.

WE'RE CHARGED WITH *INVESTIGATING* THE HOMEWORLD BEFORE RETURNING TO EARTH.

"NEVER KNOW WHAT YOU MIGHT FIND. IF THEIR HOMEWORLD FOLLOWS TRADITIONAL PATTERNS, THERE'S PROBABLY SOME SORT OF ECOLOGICAL *BALANCE.*

"PREDATOR. PREY. LIKE EARTH--LIKE *YOU* AND *ME.*

"THE ALIEN IS A REMARKABLE LIFE FORM, BUT IT MAY NOT BE THE *DOMINANT* SPECIES ON IT'S HOMEWORLD.

"A CORPORATION LIKE BIONATIONAL SUCCEEDS BY STAYING ONE STEP IN FRONT OF THE COMPETITION. IN FIVE YEARS THE ALIEN WILL BE OBSOLETE--*PASSE.* WE'LL NEED TO FIND NEWER, SUPERIOR BIOLOGICAL WEAPONS.

"WE'RE FISHING. YOUR MARINES ARE *BAIT.*"

WE'RE PICKING UP SOME BURN ON THE OUTER HULL-- GROUND SCANNERS ARE STARTING TO CLEAR--

JE-SUS, MASSEY--ARE YOU SEEING THIS?

YEAH. PUT DOWN NEAR THE FORMATION AND DISPATCH THE FLOATERS.

MAKE SURE ALL THE DATA RECORDERS ARE UP--THEY'RE GOING TO WANT THIS ON DISC.

THEN DROP THE MARINES AND ENJOY THE SHOW.

THE ATMOSPHERE'S MARGINAL, BUT THERE ARE ONLY ENOUGH MASKS FOR US GOOD GUYS. HELL, THOUGH, YOU'RE ROUGH, TOUGH MARINES.

YOU CAN HANDLE IT--

I STILL DON'T LIKE THIS.

COME ON--YOU READ THE DOCUMENTATION. THE ADULTS ARE A BITCH, BUT THEY'RE GROUND BASED.

ONCE THE CRABLIKE THINGS ATTACH TO A HOST, THEY GO DORMANT WE PICK THEM UP, WE GO HOME. NO PROBLEM.

YEAH, RIGHT--NO PROBLEM.

I KNEW I WOULD HAVE TO KILL THEM.

THE DUCTS WORMED THROUGH, THE SHIP SEPARATED BY AN INTRICATE NETWORK OF AUTOMATIC INTERIOR DOORS.

THE ALIENS USED SIMILAR TUNNELS TO ATTACK US ON ACHERON.

SOMEBODY PULLED THE LOADERS FROM THE MARINE'S BLASTERS. PROBABLY THAT PIECE OF SHIT STEPHENS.

I SAW WHAT WAS LEFT OF HIM SPATTERED DOWN IN THE LOADING BAY. SAVED ME THE TROUBLE.

THE INTRUDERS WERE CALM, CONFIDENT THAT THEY WERE IN COMPLETE CONTROL. DESPITE RIPLEY'S WARNINGS, HICKS AND HIS MARINES MADE A SIMILAR MISTAKE ON ACHERON.

IT WAS A MATTER OF PERCEPTION. THE ALIENS WOULD HAVE UNDERSTOOD.

THE BENEDICT DIDN'T BELONG TO THOSE BASTARDS IN THE LOADING BAY. IT BELONGED TO ME.

I COULDN'T IMAGINE STEPHENS ACTUALLY JETTISONING THE LOADERS--HE WAS TOO PRUDENT FOR THAT.

SOUNDS LIKE GUNFIRE--

FOOM

FOOM FOOM

CRA AUNCH!

UMPOWH!

LET'S GET THE GUNS FROM THE LANDER!

I FELT THE SHIP LURCH WHEN THE LANDER SEPARATED. BUTLER HAD LEFT WITH THEM. I COULD *FEEL* IT--THE SAME WAY I COULD STILL FEEL HIS SKIN, SO GENTLE, SO WARM--

NO. *FORGET* BUTLER. FORGET *EVERYTHING* GOOD.

CAPTAIN STEPHENS

THE ALIENS DIDN'T *NEED* LOVE. LONELINESS--FEAR--THE CONCEPTS WERE MEANINGLESS.

THEY ONLY KNEW DEATH. IT KEPT THINGS *SIMPLE.*

KA-CHUNK

119

120

WELL. WE SEEM TO HAVE MISSED ONE.

WHAT ARE YOU? SHIP'S MASCOT?

RELEASE HICKS. NOW.

THE ALIEN WOULD HAVE ATTACKED. WHAT WAS WRONG WITH ME? WHY COULDN'T I FIRE?

I-- I SAID RELEASE HIM.

YOU'RE VERY PRETTY. YOU CAN'T BE ONE OF THESE HARD-ASS MARINES.

I'LL BET YOU'VE NEVER EVEN FIRED ONE OF THOSE TH--

SHOOT HIM, NEWT!

DON'T. DON'T COME ANY CLOSER--

YOU WOULDN'T WANT TO KILL ME, HONEY.

HOW COULD YOU LIVE WITH YOURSELF-- MURDERING ANOTHER HUMAN BEING--?

IT WASN'T FAIR. I WANTED TO BE JUST LIKE THEM.

STAY BA--

GOD HELP ME. I WAS ONLY HUMAN.

--YOU STUPID BITCH--

--TRY TO USE A WEAPON AGAINST *ME*--CHRIST--

WHM

UNGHH!

I DON'T NEED *WEAPONS.* I COULD OPEN YOUR THROAT WITH MY *FINGERS*--FEEL THE BLOOD *SPRAY* DOWN MY ARMS--

--BUT YOU'RE NOT WORTH THE *EFFORT.*

YOU'RE *NOTHING*-- A *DISTRACTION*--

--CHRIST YOU REMIND ME OF MY *WIFE.*

123

125

WE LAUNCHED MASSEY'S LANDER AND BEGAN THE SLOW DESCENT TO THE ALIEN'S HOMEWORLD.

I COULD SEE BUTLER OVER THE SHIP'S MONITORS.

HIS FACE WAS REDUCED TO AN ABSTRACT BLUR--TINY ELECTRIC PULSES OF LIGHT AND COLOR

HICKS IGNORES THE SCREENS, LOST IN HIS DREAMS OF VENGEANCE. AT LEAST HE STILL HAD THAT.

I HAD NOTHING.

THERE WERE NO DREAMS LEFT FOR ME--

SHORT BURSTS, DAMN IT! CONSERVE YOUR FIRE--!

MOTION SENSORS ARE OFF THE SCALE-- THEY'RE ALL OVER US--!

BRRAKKK

BOOM BOOM

--JUST THE STARK REALITY OF THE ALIEN--

KRAAPP!

MOVE IT!

--THE STARK REALITY OF *DEATH*--

I'M READING PLUS 200 ROUNDS, BUTLER--WE'RE RUNNING OUT OF TIME!

THEY'RE CONVERGING AHEAD--AS IF THEY'RE SWARMING OVER SOME--

BRRP!

FOOM

BLAM!

OH MY GOD--

--IN HERE-- NOW!

FOOM

PLEASE-- K--KEEP THEM AWAY--

THE REST ARE *DEAD.* BURN THESE ALIEN BASTARDS AND THEN *BACK* OUT--

BLAM BLAM BLAM

--MAYBE ONE OR TWO OF US WILL ACTUALLY MAKE IT IN ONE *PIECE*--

HICKS DROPPED THE LANDER JUST OUTSIDE THE ALIEN HIVE. SAND AND DUST DANCED AROUND THE SHIP LIKE SOME MOCKING, ETHEREAL *SMOKE*--

--LIKE PHOSPHORESCENT SWIRLS OF COLOR FLICKERING ACROSS THE LANDER'S FORWARD *MONITOR*.

DAMN IT, BUTLER, DON'T FALL BACK--!

JUST KEEP MOVING--

I THINK IT *KNEW*. I THINK IT WANTED TO TEACH ME A *LESSON* ABOUT THE FUTILITY OF LOVE--THE HORROR OF *TRUST*--

I'LL COVER--

--I COULD SEE IT *ALL*--

AGGGGGHHHH--

NEWT--
STOP IT!

DAMN IT, NEWT--I TRIED TO KEEP YOU AWAY FROM HIM-- FROM *ALL* OF THEM--

WHY DO YOU THINK THEY WENT BACK FOR THOSE BASTARDS IN THE HIVE? THEIR PRINCIPAL FUNCTION IS TO PRESERVE LIFE. *HUMAN* LIFE.

THEY WERE--*ENGINEERED*--JUST FOR THIS MISSION. SPENT THEIR WHOLE LIVES LOCKED INSIDE THAT MARINE COMPOUND, WAITING FOR *THIS* MOMENT.

THEY'RE COST EFFICIENT AND *EXPENDABLE.* YOU, ME, STEVENS--WE WERE THE ONLY HUMANS ON BOARD.

THERE WERE INTERACTION PROBLEMS WITH EARLIER MODELS--HUMANS JUST DIDN'T *LIKE* THEM, SO THESE PROTOTYPES WERE DESIGNED TO *SOCIALIZE--* THEY *EAT* LIKE US, *TALK* LIKE US--

DAMNED PROGRAMMERS WERE ALMOST *TOO* CLEVER. THE ANDROIDS DEVELOPED *SENSITIVITIES.* THERE WERE QUESTIONS ABOUT THEIR EMOTIONAL *STABILITY--*HOW THEY'D REACT TO THE TRUTH--

--SO WE TREATED THEM AS *EQUALS--* PLAYED ALONG WITH THE DECEPTION--

STEPHENS WAS TRYING TO TELL THOSE BASTARDS JUST BEFORE THEY KILLED HIM-- THE ALIENS NEED *LIVING* TISSUE TO INCUBATE-- "BAIT." *THAT'S* A LAUGH.

WHY-- DIDN'T YOU-- TELL *ME*?

CHRIST, NEWT, YOU WEREN'T SUPPOSED TO FALL IN *LOVE* WITH THEM-- I COULDN'T JEOPARDIZE THE *MISSION* JUST FOR *YOU*--

YOU'RE WORSE THAN *ANY* OF THEM. YOU'RE *DEAD* INSIDE-- JUST *LIKE* THE ALIENS-- LIKE THAT SON OF A BITCH I *SHOT*--

TO THINK I WANTED TO BE LIKE YOU--

NEWT--

FWOM!

PWM!!

GET INSIDE AND LOCK DOWN--

HURRY--!

PWM, PWM!! FWOM!

HICKS-- THE HATCH IS SEALED-- EVERYONE'S ABOARD--

FORGET THE ALIENS-- WE HAVE TO *LAUNCH!*

KA-WHMM!

--NOT UNTIL I SET THE WARHEADS--

131

DON'T--
DON'T LOOK
AT ME--

YOU
MUST HAVE
KNOWN. HOW
COULD YOU--
WE--
HAVE--

DOES IT
MATTER? DOES
ANYTHING MATTER
ANYMORE?

JUST DON'T--
LEAVE ME-- LET
ME PRETEND
A FEW MORE
SECONDS--

YEAH--
COME TO PAPA,
YOU SON OF A
BITCH--

SCRREEEEEK

SAVE IT
FOR THE REST
OF US--

--I'LL
DIE BEFORE
I LET THEM
TOUCH ME
AG--

IT HAD *DEAD EYES*, SEEING AND *NOT* SEEING.

IT HAD *DESTROYED* THE ALIENS, BUT NOT FOR US. *NEVER* FOR US.

WHY?

IT DIDN'T *SPEAK*, BUT SOMETHING *EXPLODED* INSIDE MY HEAD, BRIGHT LIKE A MILLION *SUNS*--

THE IMAGES BOILED UP FROM SOME *DEEPER* PLACE, THE SAME PLANE AS PRIMAL *INSTINCT*-- HUNGER, PAIN, FEAR--

--HATRED.

NEWT--!

I-- CAN-- SEE--

MY NAME IS REBECCA, BUT EVERYONE CALLS ME NEWT. I'M SIX YEARS OLD. I LIVE ON A WORLD CALLED ACHERON.

THERE ARE 159 OF US ON THE PLANET. THE CORPORATION CALLS US TERRAFORMERS. MY FATHER CALLS US PIONEERS.

THE CORPORATION HAD SENT US OUT TO INVESTIGATE SOME SORT OF MAGNETIC SURGE. I CAN STILL REMEMBER MY FATHER'S SMILE-- THE SCENT OF MY MOTHER'S PERFUME--

THE READINGS ARE GOING OFF SCALE-- WE MUST HAVE FOUND THE MOTHER LODE--!

--AND YOU KNOW THE RULES-- WE FIND IT, WE KEEP IT.

--MY GOD.

HARD TO BELIEVE SOMETHING THIS BIG--WITH THIS KIND OF RESONANCE-- WENT WITHOUT BEING NOTICED--

IT'S PARTLY SHELTERED BY NATURAL ROCK FORMATIONS--AND THE DAMNED EC-SATS NEVER WORKED UP TO SPEC--

WHAT'S IT MATTER? IT'S OURS NOW.

MY NAME'S NEWT--I--I'M NOT SIX YEARS OLD--JESUS, IT WAS ALL SO LONG AGO. I DON'T WANT TO REMEMBER. DON'T MAKE ME REMEMBER.

WIND'S REALLY KICKING UP--WE'LL MAKE A QUICK LOOP TO SECURE THE CLAIM, THEN HEAD BACK--

--MY GOD, RUSS--IT'S ENORMOUS--

YOU KIDS STAY INSIDE I MEAN IT-- NO FOOLING AROUND.

YOU CAN WATCH OVER THE MONITOR, BUT DON'T TOUCH.

OVER HERE-- LOOKS LIKE SOME SORT OF GASH IN THE HULL--

I CAN'T STAND TO SEE IT HAPPEN AGAIN.

I WAS ONLY SIX YEARS OLD. THE DISCOVERY OF THE DERELICT DIDN'T REALLY MEAN ANYTHING TO ME.

WE HAD BATTLED TIME, SPACE, THE ELEMENTS-- AND WON. WE WEREN'T AFRAID.

--THIS IS INCREDIBLE-- EVERYTHING'S SMOOTH, ALMOST ORGANIC--

--ANNE-- --IN HERE--!

WE HAD TERRAFORMED A BARREN ROCK INTO A VIABLE, LIFE-SUSTAINING PLANET.

THAT CAME LATER.

MAYBE THAT THING IN THE DERELICT SHARED OUR BLIND ARROGANCE--

--UNTIL THE ALIENS KILLED IT.

137

IT SOMEHOW *KNEW* THAT I HAD SEEN THE WRECKAGE. WE SHARED A GROTESQUE FORM OF *EMPATHY*--

NEWT--WHAT'S IT *DOING* TO YOU?

UKKK-- IT--WANTS ME TO *KNOW*--

I COULD ONLY PICK OUT BITS AND PIECES--LIKE SOMEONE BLINKING *CHANNELS* ON A VIDEO.

IT DESCRIBED A *SHIP*--SOME KIND OF *MISSION*--

THE EGGS--OH GOD-- THE EGGS--

DON'T--MAKE ME-- SEE IT--*AGAIN*--

MY NAME-- IS NEWT-- I'M SIX YEARS OLD--

--MY FATHER *KNELT*--IN FRONT OF THE PODS. I COULD SEE HIM OVER THE TRACTOR'S MONITOR-- I COULD SEE THE *EXCITEMENT* IN HIS EYES--

JESUS, ANNE, I SEE SOMETHING *MOVING*-- I THINK THEY'RE STILL *ALI*--

I COULD HEAR A HIGH PITCHED WHINE IN MY EARS, LIKE SOME DISTANT, HORRIBLE SCREAM.

THIS ANTENNA'S SHOT. WE'LL HAVE TO BYPASS IT AND RUN THE DIRECTIONALS THROUGH THE AFT SYSTEM.

MY MIND WAS SLIPPING AWAY.

WHEN YOU'RE YOUNG, YOU CAN'T UNDERSTAND EVIL. IT'S AN INTANGIBLE THING--LIKE THE AIR OR THE SKY--

I WANTED TO BELIEVE THERE WAS SOMETHING BETTER--THAT THERE WAS SOME KIND OF HOPE.

--AND JUST AS PERVASIVE.

IT WATCHED US WITH IT'S DEAD EYES AND I FELT A CHILL. IT HAD COME TO THE ALIEN HOME-WORLD OUT OF HATE. IT HAD RESCUED US IN THE NAME OF REVENGE.

PERHAPS EVIL IS THE ONLY UNIVERSAL TRUTH.

EYES ONLY
DOUBLE A-ALPHA
LOG ON, ORONA.

I-I'VE LOST
TRACK OF TIME SINCE
THE BIONATIONAL ATTACK
I'VE BARRACADED MYSELF
IN MY OFFICE TO GIVE ME
TIME TO PREPARE THIS
FINAL REPORT.

EVIDENTLY THE ALIEN
QUEEN IS ABLE TO
COMMUNICATE IN SOME
SUBCONSCIOUS
FASHION, WITH OTHER
SPECIES. IN HUMAN
BEINGS, THESE
DISSEMINATIONS
MANIFEST THEMSELVES
IN THE FORM OF
PATTERN NIGHTMARES.

THE DREAMS WERE
A LURE.

AT FIRST WE THOUGHT
WE'D BE ABLE TO
CONTAIN THE SPORE.
INFESTATION SEEMED
LIMITED TO A
NARROW GEOGRAPHIC
RANGE.

BLAM! BLAM!

BRRRP!

AAGH...!

AND YET FOR EVERY CLUSTER
WE FOUND, THERE WERE TEN
MORE JUST LIKE IT.

NAME'S OSTROW.
LOOKS LIKE HE WAS
SOME SORT OF BIG SHOT
WITH BIONATIONAL.

BURN
THE SON
OF A
BITCH.

THE ALIEN'S SUBCONSCIOUS *BAIT* TRANSCENDED CLASS AND POLITICAL BOUNDARIES. WE FOUND HIVES *EVERYWHERE.*

COME ON, MOVE IT!

I WANT A PERIMETER AROUND THE HOUSE AND I WANT AIR SUPPORT, *NOW--!*

WITH EACH NEW DISCOVERY, OUR HOPE OF DESTROYING THE CREATURES BEFORE THEY ENTERED THE CIVILIAN POPULATION *FADED.*

POOM

HOWEVER WE STILL CONSIDERED *CONTAINMENT* AN OPTION. IN STUDYING THE BIONATIONAL FILES WE LEARNED THEIR QUEEN HAD GESTATED A NUMBER OF *WEEKS* PRIOR TO MATURATION.

USING THEIR EXPERIMENT AS A BASELINE, I ASSUMED WE STILL HAD TIME BEFORE ANY NEW QUEENS WOULD BECOME *VIABLE.*

I WAS *WRONG.*

PERHAPS OUR WORST MISTAKE WAS UNDERESTIMATING THE SHEER INSTINCTUAL *CUNNING* OF THE CREATURES. WE DIDN'T SEE THE UNDERLYING *PATTERN* BEHIND THEIR EVOLUTIONARY PROCESS--THE WAY EVERY FACET OF THEIR EXISTANCE WAS GEARED TOWARD *PROPAGATION.* THE QUEENS MATURED AT WHATEVER SPEED THEIR *SURVIVAL* DICTATED.

WE HAD ASSUMED THE GESTATION PERIOD WAS TIME FOR THE ALIEN EMBRYO TO FEED AND GROW, BUT IT WAS MORE THAN THAT. IT WAS AN OPPORTUNITY FOR THE UNKNOWING *HOST* TO SPREAD IT'S *SPORE* TO OTHER SITES.

THERE WAS A GEOMETRIC *PERFECTION* TO THE INFESTATIONS.

EACH QUEEN WOULD LAY STILL *MORE* QUEENS, AND WITH EVERY GENERATION THE SPORE BECAME MORE ENTRENCHED, MORE--

WHUMP!

AHH. AT LAST.

THE CIVILIAN AUTHORITY WAS WEAK IN THE FACE OF THE DEVASTATION. WHEN THE GENERALS FINALLY STAGED THEIR COUP IT SEEMED ALMOST--*WELCOME.*

AGHH-- YOU CAN'T DO THIS-- IT'S AGAINST THE--

SHUT UP!

THE MILITARY CREATED TESTING CENTERS WHERE PHYSICIANS CHECKED CIVILIANS FOR SIGNS OF THE ALIEN INFECTION. AT FIRST THE TESTS WERE VOLUNTARY.

Testing CENTER →

WITHIN DAYS THAT *CHANGED.*

THERE WERE RUMORS THE MILITARY WAS USING THE PRETEXT OF ALIEN INFECTION TO *ELIMINATE* POLITICAL DISSIDENTS--THE POOR, THE DISAFFECTED--

AS IF SUCH PETTY RIVALRIES EVEN *MATTERED.*

VITAL SERVICES-- WATER, ELECTRICITY-- BEGAN TO *FAIL*.

WE'VE HEARD OF INFESTATIONS IN EUROPE, AUSTRALIA. THE SEED IS GROWING WITH REMARKABLE SPEED.

FROM ALL THIS, I'VE COME TO *UNDERSTAND* SOMETHING ABOUT HUMANITY.

MAN IS AN ANIMAL, DRIVEN BY ANIMAL PASSIONS. 'CIVILIZATION' IS A PATHETIC CHARADE OF *MANNERS*, PREDICATED ON A TISSUE-THIN VEIL OF *LIES*.

IN THE FUTURE-- IF THERE *IS* A FUTURE-- HISTORIANS MAY BLAME OUR FAILURES ON SOME *EXTERNAL CAUSE*--

--THE ALIENS. BINATIONAL. *FATE*.

I KNOW THE TRUTH. THOSE *THINGS* DIDN'T DESTROY US.

WE DID.

THEY-- THEY'LL BE *HERE* SOON.

THE MILITARY HAS ORGANIZED OFF-WORLD SHIPS TO EVACUATE "VITAL PERSONNEL" TO THE OUTER COLONIES--MAINLY THEIR *OWN* PRECIOUS HIDES.

I'VE CHOSEN TO REMAIN BEHIND.

WE MADE THE MISTAKE OF PERCEIVING THE ALIENS AS SENTIENT *WARRIORS*. I FINALLY REALIZED THE TRUTH. THEY'RE *DISEASE*. A CANCER.

IT'LL BE JUST A MOMENT, COLONEL. THE SEALS HAVE TO BE BURNED BEFORE THE OUTER DOOR--

YEARS AGO, FOLLOWING SURGERY, DOCTORS WOULD APPLY *RADIATION* TO THE AFFECTED AREA IN HOPE OF DESTROYING ALL TRACES OF THE SCOURGE.

U.S. ... KEEP OUT

JUST DO IT.

I'M SHOWING GREEN ON 90% OF THE WARHEADS. THE BURST SHOULD VAPORIZE THE MOUNTAIN-- PREVAILING WINDS WILL DO THE REST--

MY-- MY *MOTHER* DIED OF CANCER. ODD HOW I'VE BEEN *THINKING* OF HER--

IT SOUNDS SO PRIMITIVE, BUT THERE ARE TIMES WHEN THE OLD WAYS ARE MOST EFFECTIVE.

146

I'VE TIMED THE DETONATION TO COINCIDE WITH THE MILITARY'S *ESCAPE*!

THEY THINK THEY CAN *DESTROY* THE CREATURES. THEY THINK SOMEDAY THEY'LL BE ABLE TO *COME BACK* TO THEIR WORLD.

THERE'S SOMETHING *PATHETIC* ABOUT THE STRUGGLE. MY ONLY REGRET IS THAT I WON'T SURVIVE TO SEE THEM PROVEN *WRONG*.

I TAKE PRIDE IN MY *PRAGMATISM*-- I REALIZE THIS TRANSMISSION IS POINTLESS. I DOUBT IF THE LONG RANGE RELAY STATIONS ARE EVEN *OPERATIONAL*--

STILL-- IF ANYONE IS ACTUALLY *SEEING* THIS-- I JUST-- I--

DOESN'T REALLY MATTER DOES IT? I'VE NEVER ACTUALLY *FIRED* ONE OF THESE--I FEEL RATHER--

SCRUNCH

--FOOLISH.

BDAM!

OH GOD, NO--!

148

DESTROYING THE ALIENS HAD BEEN AN ALL CONSUMING PASSION, YET THERE WAS LITTLE SENSE OF *ACHIEVEMENT* AS WE LEFT TO RENDEZVOUS WITH THE BENEDICT.

HICKS WENT THROUGH THE MOTIONS BECAUSE "THE MOTIONS" WERE ALL WE HAD LEFT.

THE "OTHER" WATCHED AND APPROVED, AND IN THE END, REVENGE WAS JUST ANOTHER CHEMICAL *REACTION*--LIKE *ALL* THINGS IN LIFE--

ONE INSTANT, THE HIVE WAS THERE.

THE NEXT INSTANT, IT WAS GONE.

FINALLY, HICKS KNEW HE *HAD* TO GO BACK. THERE SIMPLY WASN'T ANYTHING *ELSE*.

COURSE ENTERED, GRAVITY DRIVE UP--

LET'S GET THE HELL OUT OF HERE.

WE WERE *NOTHING* WHEN WE LEFT EARTH. WE'D BEEN SENT TO FIND SPECIMENS. WE WERE RETURNING WITH *SALVATION.*

THE WORD SEEMED HOLLOW, *RIDICULOUS.* WHERE WOULD I FIND *MY* SALVATION?

--BUTLER?

DON'T-- PLEASE--

ARE YOU--ARE YOU ALRIGHT?

PLEASE, NEWT--DON'T *LOOK* AT ME--

I--I CAN'T. I NEED TO KNOW.

I NEED TO KNOW IF--IF WHAT WE HAD WAS *REAL.*

WHEN THAT--*THING* TORE INTO ME-- I REMEMBER THINKING HOW MUCH I *LOVED* YOU--

--THEN I SAW WHAT WAS *LEFT*--AND SUDDENLY I KNEW--

--GOD WE *ALL* KNEW--

HICKS SAID IT WAS JUST *PROGRAMMING*--PART OF SOME SOCIALIZATION PROCESS--YOU BELIEVED YOU WERE HUMAN BECAUSE IT WAS *EASIER*--

BUT THAT DOESN'T EXPLAIN WHAT HAPPENED BETWEEN US. IT *CAN'T.*

IT-- CAN'T--

I--I TOUCHED HIM. HIS SKIN WAS WARM--SOFT.

HE WAS ALIVE.

MAYBE ALL LIFE IS LIKE HICKS' REVENGE-- CHEMICAL-- RANDOM--

--HATE--DEATH--LOVE-- ALL MEANINGLESS OUTSIDE SOME LARGER CONTEXT--

--IT ALWAYS COMES BACK TO OUR ARROGANCE. THE SCIENTISTS WANT TO DRAW A LINE BETWEEN MAN AND HIS MACHINES--

NEWT--

--BUT WHAT DID IT MATTER? BUTLER CARED FOR ME. NOT LIKE HICKS--NOT LIKE EARTH'S DOCTORS--

WHAT MADE THEIR HATE MORE ALIVE THAN THEIR CREATION'S LOVE?

TIME PASSED QUICKLY. FOR THE FIRST TIME SINCE ACHERON, I FELT A SENSE OF CALM.

EARTH DRIFTED BELOW US LIKE SOME BRIGHT TOY AND AT LONG LAST WE WERE HOME.

WE HAVEN'T GOT MUCH TIME. THE CREATURES HAVE *BREACHED* THE GALVESTON SECURITY LINE--I THOUGHT ORONA SAID--

ORONA'S *DEAD*--! HAPPENED *WEEKS* AGO-- WE FOUND WHAT WAS LEFT OF HIM INSIDE THE MAIN BIO LAB--

SIR--WE'RE PICKING UP *TWO* SHIPS ON THE DS SCANNER-- ONE'S EMITTING A STANDARD TYPE FOUR BEACON--THE OTHER IS UNIDENTIFIED--

THE TYPE FOUR'S ASKING PERMISSION TO LAND. WE'VE CANNIBALIZED MOST OF THE TRANSCODE COMPUTERS, BUT I MANAGED TO PULL A PRELIMINARY I.D.--

THE BENEDICT--MY GOD-- STEPHEN'S SHIP--

GRANT PERMISSION FOR LANDING. I'LL MEET THEM AT THE PAD *PERSONALLY*--

WIND AND RAIN BATTERED THE SHIP AS WE SETTLED ON THE LANDING PLATFORM. IT WAS ALMOST AS IF NATURE ITSELF WERE REBELLING AGAINST THE MILITARY'S PLAN.

THE RAIN REMINDED ME OF ACHERON--REMINDED ME OF MY *INNOCENCE*--

TAKE THE SYNTHETICS TO REHAB--WE'LL DEAL WITH THEM *LATER*--

--ONE OF THE BIONATIONAL EXECUTIVES TOLD US ABOUT STEPHENS AFTER ALL THE *SHIT* CAME DOWN--

--*YOU* WON'T HAVE TO WORRY ABOUT THOSE BASTARDS ANY--

DAMN IT, *LISTEN TO ME*-- ORONA TRANSMITTED A MESSAGE ABOUT THE *DETONATION* JUST BEFORE HE DIED. YOU HAVE TO STOP IT--

"--THERE MAY BE ANOTHER WAY--"

--WE'VE SUSPECTED THE EXISTENCE OF OTHER SENTIENT BEINGS SINCE THE NOSTROMO MISSION. IT DOESN'T *CHANGE* THINGS.

THE ALIENS HAVE *WON*, CORPORAL. BASIC MILITARY TACTICS--WHEN YOU'RE OUTGUNNED, YOU *RETREAT*--AND LEAVE *NOTHING* FOR YOUR ENEMY.

JESUS--HAVEN'T YOU HEARD ANYTHING I'VE *SAID?* THERE'S STILL A CHANCE IF YOU'LL *DEAL* WITH THE--

TH-THEY DON'T *WANT* TO STOP IT.

WHAT--?

IT'S ONLY A MATTER OF TIME BEFORE THE ALIENS OVERRUN US-- WE'VE GOT TO DEAL WITH THE *REALITY* OF THE SITUATION--

ORONA UNDERSTOOD. THE ALIEN ATTACK ISN'T EVIL. IT'S *OPPORTUNITY*--

154

"--EARTH'S BEEN ON THE BRINK OF DESTRUCTION FOR DECADES. THERE'S NO *DISCIPLINE*-- NO *ORDER*.

"THE ALIENS ONLY *EXACERBATED* THE SITUATION. IT WOULD HAVE COME TO THIS SOONER OR LATER.

"IT'S A CHANCE TO *CLEAN THE SLATE*-- A CHANCE TO START AGAIN--

"AFTER A FEW YEARS--WHEN IT'S OVER-- THE SURVIVORS CAN RETURN AND TERRAFORM EARTH INTO SOMETHING *BEAUTIFUL* AGAIN--

"ORONA UNDERSTOOD-- THE ALIENS HAVE GIVEN US A CHANCE TO *REDISCOVER* OURSELVES--

"IT'S A *GOOD* THING."

FOR THE FIRST TIME SINCE *ACHERON*, I *LAUGHED*. I LAUGHED BECAUSE *WORDS* HAD LOST THEIR MEANING-- BECAUSE THAT *SON OF A BITCH* ORONA HAD BEEN *RIGHT*--

--THE ALIENS *DIDN'T* DESTROY US--

--*WE* DID.

SIR--THERE'S BEEN A *BREECH* OF THE SOUTHERN PERIMETER OUR SPOTTERS HAVE SEEN *HUNDREDS* OF THE--

LOCK DOWN THE SHIPS AND PREPARE FOR LAUNCH. IT'S *TIME*.

AND WHAT ABOUT *US*--?

YOU DID WHAT YOU THOUGHT WAS RIGHT. THE TIME FOR MILITARY PROTOCOL AND POLITE INQUIRIES ARE LONG PAST--

--YOU'RE LIKE EVERYONE ELSE STILL ON EARTH. *UNNECESSARY!*

--BACK AWAY-- REPORT TO THE PAD FOR LAUNCH--!

BRRR!

UNNECESSARY MY ASS.

JUST LET IT END. THE WAY IT SHOULD HAVE ENDED ON *ACHERON*-- FOR *BOTH* OF US--

--I'M NOT GIVING THOSE ALIEN SHITS THE *PLEASURE* AND NEITHER ARE *YOU*--

I SMUGGLED YOU ABOARD THE BENEDICT-- AND IF I'VE LEARNED ONE THING ABOUT THE MILITARY IT'S *THIS*--

THEY NEVER LEARN--

LEVEL 1

KEANU LAB

WAIT--!

WE DON'T HAVE *TIME* FOR THIS, NEWT--

THIS IS WHERE THEY TOOK *BUTLER*--I--

THEY *DESTROYED* THE OTHERS--TOOK WHAT THEY COULD *SALVAGE*--

I--I DIDN'T THINK YOU'D COME *BACK*.

OH GOD-- WHAT HAVE THEY *DONE*--?

156

--HALF THESE SHIPS ARE AUTOMATED CARGO CARRIERS--NO *CREW*. IF WE CAN IDENTIFY A SPECIFIC--

--THAT'S IT. DECK FOUR.

KEEP FIRING! KEEP FIRING! WE CAN'T LET THEM GET TO THE PAD--

--WE CAN'T LE--

BRRAP!

FOOM! FOOM!

I'M STILL NOT SURE WHAT HICKS WAS THINKING AS WE CLIMBED ABOARD THE CARGO SHIP. PERHAPS HE WASN'T *THINKING* AT ALL--JUST *REACTING* AS THE SOLDIER IN HIM TOOK OVER--

THE AMERICAN

DAMN IT, HURRY!

AAAGGGG--

--OR MAYBE AFTER ALL THE DEATH AND PAIN, SOMETHING FINALLY *SPARKED* INSIDE HIM SOMETHING *PRECIOUS*.

--WE GOT *LUCKY* MOST OF THESE CARGO JOBS HAVE BEEN RETROFITTED FOR TOTAL AUTO OPERATION. THIS ONE STILL HAS SOME *MANUAL* CONTROLS.

--FULLY PRESSURIZED ATMOSPHERE'S NOMINAL--MAKES SENSE--

--SHIP'S REGISTER SPECIFIES ORGANIC CARGO HELL--IT'S NOAH'S HAPPY LITTLE ARK.

HIS WILL TO *LIVE*.

--THE ALIENS HAVE ENTERED THE *FACILITY*-- PREPARE THE SHIPS FOR LAUNCH ON *MY* COMMAND--

--SIR-- SOME OF THE MEN ARE STILL ON *DECK*, MAKING FINAL--

--I'M PROUD OF EVERY ONE OF THEM. NOW PREPARE FOR LAUNCH OR I'LL HAVE YOU *SHOT.*

I COULD HEAR GUNFIRE AND *SCREAMS* AS THE ALIENS ADVANCED ON OUR SHIP. THE SOUNDS OF A PLANET DYING.

THE AUTOMATIC LAUNCH SEQUENCERS LOCKED AND THE WHINE OF THE SHIP'S ENGINES DROWNED OUT THE HORROR BELOW.

WE WERE LEAVING EARTH TO THE ALIENS AND ORONA'S 'OPPORTUNITY'--

I SUPPOSE I SHOULD HAVE CRIED-- FELT *SOMETHING* FOR THOSE WE LEFT BEHIND--BUT I'D RUN OUT OF TEARS *LONG* AGO--

--AND THEN IT *SPOKE* TO ME--

--SOMETHING EXPLODED--BRIGHT, LIKE A MILLION *SUNS*--

I-- CAN-- SEE--

NEWT-- WHAT'S WRONG--?

IT--IT HAD *CHANGED* SINCE THE HOMEWORLD IT TOOK ME A MOMENT TO FULLY COMPREHEND--

AGGHH--

IT *UNDERSTOOD* ABOUT ORONA-- IT *KNEW* HIS TWISTED PLAN--

WE THOUGHT IT *SHARED* OUR THIRST FOR *VENGEANCE.* WE LED IT TO EARTH IN THE MISTAKEN BELIEF IT MIGHT WANT TO "HELP" US.

HOW COULD WE HAVE BEEN SO *BLIND?* IT SHARED SO MANY OF OUR MERCURIAL HUMAN EMOTIONS. HATE. ANGER.

IT JUST WANTED ME TO *KNOW.*

THE DESIRE TO *CONQUER.*

IT NO LONGER *CARED* ABOUT THE ALIENS. INTEREST HAD *SHIFTED.* THE SOLDIERS ASSUMED THEY WOULD RETURN ONE DAY AND TERRAFORM EARTH FOR *THEMSELVES*--

IT WOULD *WATCH.* IT WOULD BE *WAITING* FOR THEM.

THE CARGO VESSEL'S NAVIGATIONAL COMPUTERS WERE LOCKED ONTO A DEEP SPACE TRAJECTORY. THE GRAVITY DRIVE PULSED LIKE A LIVING THING, PROPELLING US ACROSS BILLIONS OF MILES OF SPACE.

HICKS FINALLY HAD HIS REVENGE, BUT HE FOUND NO *SATISFACTION* IN IT.

WHEN IT BEGAN, HE BLAMED HIS MISERY ON THE *ALIENS*. NOW ALL HE COULD BLAME WAS *HIMSELF*.

I WAS STANDING AT ONE OF THE VIEWPORTS, STARING INTO SPACE. THE LIGHT FROM THE STARS STRETCHED AROUND THE SHIP LIKE GLOWING WHITE NEON--

--BUT THIS TIME IT WAS *DIFFERENT*.

I WASN'T *ALONE* ANYMORE-- AND MAYBE, FINALLY, THAT WAS ALL THAT *MATTERED*.